First published 2023

ISBN: 97988516.

Copyright © Max de Grussa 2023

The right of Max de Grussa to be identified as the author of this work has been asserted by him in accordance with the Copyright, Designs and Patents Act 1988.

All rights reserved. No part of this publication may be reproduced, stored in a retrievable system, or transmitted in any form, or by any means (electronic, mechanical, photocopying, recording or otherwise) without the prior written permission of the publisher.

Amazon does not have any control over, or any responsibility for, any author or third party websites referred to in this book.

This book is sold subject to the condition that it shall not, by way of trade or otherwise, be lent, hired out, or otherwise circulated without the publisher's prior consent in any form of binding or cover other than that in which it is published and without a similar condition including this condition being imposed on the subsequent purchaser.

FOR

Angelique, Colette and Jacqueline

ACKNOWLEDGEMENTS

To all those in my bubble.

1

Henry Drax stood looking out the hospital window with unseeing eyes. The wet blackened chimmnied rooftops and dotted parkland expanded into the endless dull grey landscape severed by the silver Thames River snaking its way towards the sea, oppressed by an even greyer sky. It made no impression on Henry nor did the well-lit bustling hospital with its distinct antiseptic odours and distasteful surrounding green and cream walls. Immersed in his thoughts of the overwhelming events that seemed to have developed suddenly in his life but in fact had been simmering during the war years, had now come home to roost. What he faced was the end result, years of stagnation and post war poverty, putting, what was a pre-war thriving business, founded by his father Reginald, at risk. Henry, experienced in finance, risk assessment and management, had now become a victim of the war or at least the business had. He was not really a good businessman and like everyone else could not have foreseen what was coming or what the end result would be. After years of fighting to defeat the Nazi oppressors, victory meant national bankruptcy and poverty. The accounting firm Maddison & Chapman he inherited after his father, who through no fault of his own was vaporised in the first London bombing raid when a bomb dropped by the Luftwaffe in 1940 landed three feet in front of Reginald Drax while he was on his way to see a client in Whitehall. The only identifying evidence was the lid from his briefcase that had his name and address inside whereas everything else including Reginald had been converted to nothing. Henry didn't much care for his father who had press-ganged Henry, against his wishes, into the business. But after becoming the managing director, following his father's untimely death, Henry quickly learnt to enjoy the status and trappings. However, the business was plunged into difficulties as focus had been on servicing the war effort, which ceased immediately after VE day. He was struggling to rebuild a healthy level of private clients to keep the business afloat and had succumbed to some suspect dealings that had damaged Maddison & Chapman's reputation. He needed to quickly find something to stop the company going into administration, desperate times require desperate measures.

'Henry!'

Henry was jolted out of his thoughts and slowly turned to face the woman in the hospital bed. A comfortable bed in a private room in Teddington Memorial Hospital only the best, always the best she expected, demanded, after all his wife is a Westwood.

'Sorry Rosemary, miles away' responded Henry 'what did you say'

'Are you pleased with Anthony?'

Henry looked at the bundle Rosemary was holding. Rosemary is thirty-two and he twenty-seven for God's sake. He didn't want a child, never did, especially now with all crumbling around him. Rosemary wanted the child, even desperate for it. By the time Anthony is twenty-one Henry will be forty-eight and he was sure that even at that age he still would not want a son. All he wanted was cut and thrust of the finance industry unless some unplanned event changed his destiny that is. He didn't want to be a father. He didn't want a son or any child, as he didn't envisage being able to commit time to the task of father anyway. There was so much to sort out. Everything had to get back on track. At least the baby would be a welcome distraction for Rosemary and free him from the constant nagging he seemed to be subjected to.

'Yes, of course dear, he will no doubt add a positive dimension to our lives. A real asset.'

'A real asset?' Rosemary said quietly. Henry could be so impersonal, void of emotion. He no doubt saw Anthony as an entry on a balance sheet. She understood his self-centered personality, a paternal trait that included an infrequent bad temper. Henry suffered general sullenness that was worse when fueled by any frustration that impacted on his life not of his making.

She knew the only positive outcome of having Anthony would be for her but she was happy with this. She would at last have someone to love and care for, someone who would in return love her. Anthony would give her purpose and she would see to it that he developed into a well-adjusted person who was strong, independent and caring.

Anthony was oblivious to anything other than sleeping at that moment, still getting over the trauma of his birth from the warm secure womb into the world at large that will be his home for the next eighty or so years. The journey had begun. He had strong genes inherited from his father and mother, mostly from his father and of course from his grandfather. Traits that unbeknown to him would be his downfall.

❖

The Bentley Mark VI glided along Twickenham Road drawing into a driveway where it confronted old rusting wrought iron gates. Henry got out of the car and opened the gates noting that something should be done to restore them. They drove up to the elegant Victorian Westwood House that having survived the incessant bombing stood proud, boasting a large expanse of lawn leading down to the Thames waterfront with a private jetty where a deteriorating clinker dinghy, was moored. The self-contained servants quarters, integral to the house, had been refurbished for Heather Westwood, Rosemary's mother, where she existed as a semi-recluse. It was the Westwood house along with the car and everything else in and around the house that Heather had inherited. Heather never really got over the death of her husband Major Robert Westwood who had served with distinction, in supply for the duration of the Great War. Robert had been awarded the Distinguished Conduct Medal that now resided in the bureau draw with Pip, Squeak and Wilfred. The irony was that a runaway lorry unceremoniously ran over and killed Robert four weeks after repatriation. To make matters worse Rosemary's younger brother Phillip had been killed in 1944 when his Spitfire was shot down over the channel. Neither the Spitfire nor Phillip were recovered.

The effect of these losses was devastating for Heather and having an irreversible psychological impact on Rosemary that she had leaned to suppress. The mix of Westwood assets and family misfortune was the environment into which Anthony was thrust. Henry was responsible to provide the revenue to keep Westwood House and its occupants in a lifestyle that was expected, something he silently objected to.

It was in 1939 that Henry and Rosemary met. Captain Henry Drax and Private Rosemary Westwood met at Lilly's cafe. Captain Drax was seconded to the Ministry of Supply based at Shell Mex House on the Strand and Private Westwood of the Women's Auxiliary Territorial Service, a driver attached to the Ministry of Supply, mostly worked out of Shell Mex House. It was there that Henry first noticed Rosemary and later when he walked into Lilly's Cafe on Carting Lane he saw her sitting alone in the cramped tearoom asking politely if he may sit at her table. It was more the common ground of their fathers having both being involved in supply, both military men and the tiresome stress of years of war that drew Henry and Rosemary together. It wasn't out of love that they married on the 4th of June 1939 but the guilt of having consummated their relationship a regular basis, with an accepted urgency in these uncertain times. Two days later Captain Drax was posted to France. However, with the death of his father Henry was repatriated to take up duties running Maddison & Chapman as it was intimately involved with the Ministry of Defence.

The first five years of Anthony's life were uneventful and secluded. With his father in London rebuilding the business and his strange withdrawn grandmother, who he curiously observed from time to time, strolling around the garden or down at the jetty staring into the deteriorating dinghy that she and Robert had built and enjoyed. When encountered, she would look at Anthony as though it was the first time she had seen him, then wander off. There was no meaningful interaction

His mother was his world. She cared for him, entertained and educated him. Gave him confidence and made him the centre of their universe. Anthony was advanced with his reading, cognitive and general communication skills for his young years and rarely played with other children, who he found tedious, even boring, so he preferred to spend his time with mother. Rosemary doted on Anthony, nurtured his independence, gaining endless pleasure in meeting his every need and want. He brought her a new dimension, meaning, to her life during the absence of Henry who spent his week in London only venturing to Teddington on the odd weekend. Rosemary and Henry's relationship was cordial and comfortable although distant with infrequent sexual encounters leaving them wondering why they did it at all. Family outings were rare and Henry's involvement with Anthony was minimal. Much of the time Henry brought work home thus spending most of his time in the study. Meal times were quiet and subdued, barely functional, something Anthony picked up at an early age and associated this change with father's presence, looking forward to his increasingly withdrawn father returning to London, hoping his next visit wouldn't be too soon. Anthony and his mother didn't discuss Henry.

❖

Norman Blakeley sat looking at the woman and child before him. How many times had he conducted such an interview that was really just a formality? The slim well-dressed woman had the look and air of breeding; after all she is a Westwood. Major Robert Westwood, the child's grandfather, was an Allard Grammar boy who, while not excelling, nevertheless did well academically and enjoyed sport, especially the rough and tumble of rugby. Robert was no trouble throughout his stay at Allard as he obeyed the rules, was of good character and generally contributing overall. Norman didn't know the boy's father although he had heard his paternal grandfather had been killed in the war. Vaporised by a bomb they said, Norman shuddered at the thought.

Norman Blakeley, the third Blakeley to make it to headmaster of this eighteen century grammar school, peered at the boy who didn't seem to have inherited the Westwood looks but showed some confidence and control.

'I am pleased you considered enrolling your son at Allard Grammar Mrs Drax' said Blakeley without conviction 'No doubt your father would have been pleased. As you know he was an Allard boy through and through.'

'My father was not a consideration Mr Blakeley. Allard was the only option, I didn't have any other thoughts on the matter.'

'Will the lad be boarding?'

'Definitely not Mr Blakeley! As you know I live only ten minutes away so there is no need especially as I do not work and have a modest social life.'

'Very well Mrs Drax we look forward to seeing your son at the start of term'

Blakeley peered again at the young boy sitting next to his mother. The boy had not uttered a word but had a fixed stare on Blakeley throughout.

'Well young man what do you think about coming to Allard Grammar?'

'Nothing Sir, I know I have to attend school and Allard

Grammar is close to home and mother.' Anthony stated. He looked with indifference at the old man on the other side of the desk. His mother said he was going to Allard Grammar like his grandfather whom he had never met and had no comprehension of such a person except in name. Anthony didn't understand school except that his mother said he must go so he would.

As Norman Blakeley ushered Mrs Drax and her son from the office he wondered about this seemingly strange confident boy but dismissed any concern against the reputation of Major Robert Westwood. However, there was something there. His intuition from years of experience was finely tuned and usually on the money.

At the start of term, Anthony Drax, in his Allard Grammar uniform, turned to look at his mother as she drove away in the Bentley towards the entrance gates. He felt nothing as he turned back to look at the school crest over the large double oak doors framed by the four stone pillars, two on either side. The Allard family crest sat above the oak doors with its motto "et serve consequi" - achieve and serve, by which the school stood steadfast.

Allard had a good reputation as the fifty-student intake each year was oversubscribed with preference given to the families to which it was alma mater, as such a history with the school had much weight. The first year students were unofficially designated 'melons' by the senior students. In fact you didn't graduate from being a 'melon' until you entered year two. The first year probationary period of being a 'melon' was no deterrent to a place at Allard that was highly prized. By the end of their schooling the aim was for each student to be a well rounded, highly educated person leading into university giving good prospects for a career in politics, commerce, finance or law. In the two hundred plus years of the school no one had been expelled or brought disgrace, a fact that Mr Blakely was proud of. At the drop of a hat he would extoll the virtues of Allard Grammar to everyone or at least to some unsuspecting person he managed to corner. Any and all 'problems' were dealt with in confidence and swept under the carpet so as not to taint the good reputation of the school. So it had always been.

Anthony entered through the large oak entrance doors into the reception hall where other new students stood around a tall slender man in a pinstriped suit. Before the First World War, as a staff member, he would have been adorned with his academic gown and square but much had changed. Mr Scott was chatting to the boys trying to put them at ease for their first day. He turned as Anthony approached.

'Hello there lad and what is your name?'

'Anthony Drax Sir'

'Hello Drax, welcome to Allard Grammar, would you stand here as there are two other boys to come.' Mr Scott marked his list surveying the boys while waiting for the latecomers. With all present Anthony and his peers walked, under the guidance of Mr Scott, into the great hall where they would be taken through procedures as part of their orientation. Later they would be split into two groups of twenty-five with each group allotted a classroom to begin their first day of school.

The Bentley was waiting when Anthony had finished his first day. His mother questioned him at length as they drove back to Westwood House.

'How was your first day of school Anthony?'

'I am not sure mother'

'Well what did you do?'

'Mr Scott explained the rules and what we will be doing over the next term. I received my study books.'

'Did you meet other boys, darling?'

'Not really mother, there are twenty five boys in my class but I didn't talk to any.'

'I am sure you will get to know them and make friends over time dear.'

'Yes mother'

So began Anthony's first academic year. The curriculum was tried and proven even though quite rigorous for the young boys. Sport was a major part of school life, which suited Anthony's highly competitive nature. As a day student he was not exposed to the full culture of Allard. Only a small portion of boys boarded with dormitories being another world altogether. Anthony wasn't interested in boarding as he enjoyed being at home with his mother who took a great interest in his studies, helping him to come to grips with overall concepts. She praised him and applauded his achievements a behaviour that nurtured his innate competitiveness and soothed his ego. Although in reality he was an above average according to school standards. He quickly learnt that other achieving students were the enemy, threatening his standing in his world, a characteristic that was picked up by boys and staff alike. To this end he was considered a potential troublemaker by the staff, although unbeknown to all he was not destined to graduate from Allard Grammar. A reserved achiever with a strong silent driven personality was the usual comment on his report that became evident by the time he had completed his first three months at Allard. Blakeley and Scott often discussed Anthony, as he wasn't cut from the same cloth as the others however they couldn't explain or justify the uneasiness they both felt and were well aware that Anthony's father took little interest in his son and he in him.

It was six months before Edward 'Teddy' Walton Matthews who was to be his only friend for the duration befriended Anthony. Teddy, a quiet loner with good family credentials somehow looked up to Anthony and followed him around.

'My father is Mr Hugh Matthews' claimed Teddy 'You know, the eminent solicitor and member of parliament.'

Anthony looked at Teddy without response.

'Grandfather and Daddy both came to Allard you know. We live at Teddington Manor and have our own motor boat.'

Teddy from Teddington Manor prattled on to the indifferent Anthony. Anthony didn't dislike Teddy; he just found him irrelevant and sometimes irritating in the world of Anthony Drax. At this early age Anthony had no interest in Teddy's claims nor understood why someone should say such things. When he told his mother about Teddy she dismissed him by reinforcing to Anthony that he would achieve a status that even the Matthews family, would be envious.

The 'melons' sporting curriculum was predominantly athletics and it was only in year four that cricket and rugby became available. Rowing was kept for the seniors and it would be well after Anthony had left that tennis was introduced.

'The Matthew family play cricket you know' continued Teddy 'Do you play cricket?'

Anthony considered cricket for a moment and wasn't sure he had ever thought about it. Although, he had seen it being played once on one of those rare occasions his father drove them to Bushy Park for a picnic. The men in their whites under the summer sun were just visible over the rear, side windowsill of the Bentley as they travelled down Glazebrook Road. Then they disappeared.

'No' responded Anthony.

Teddy prattled on.

❖

Headmaster Scott addressed the year four boys into which Anthony had graduated.

'You have all carried out your studies, sporting activities and duties well over the past three years and now you enter the next important phase of your education.'

Headmaster Blakeley had retired at the end of the previous academic year and would be the last Blakeley to ever hold the position. In fact, he and his wife had no children and there were no other Blakeley family members who had taken education as a vocation. The school board had appointed Rupert Scott in his place after considering his impressive credentials and exemplary time at Allard Grammar. Staff and students liked Scott. He had won the respect of parents and was a popular appointment.

'You will continue with your academic studies as well as having the privilege of participating in your choice of cricket or rugby. Furthermore, I am sure you will enjoy a range of excursions to broaden your education.'

'Mr Kirby will discuss your sporting preferences. Welcome to year four which comes with the same requirements for a positive attitude and duty to all. Thank you.'
'Mr Kirby.'
Rupert Scott stepped back, pleased with his first address in his new position. He had much to do so left the students to Kirby. As he made his way out of the classroom he saw Anthony Drax and was impressed that he had made it into year four although being unremarkable. Drax still had that silent determined attitude but to date there was no reason for concern.
'Right chaps' Alan Kirby took the boys attention.
Alan Ronald Kirby, since graduating in physical education, had held the sporting position at Allard purely due to being the nephew of Blakeley's wife. With his interest and bias in athletics all new boys got to know him well. Having recently married, Kirby was able to move into a small rent-free cottage in the school grounds that came with a further responsibility of being a housemaster for the eastern dormitory. A small increment in wage helped. It was a good position that he would fill until retirement, being conscientious, not ambitious.
Working through the list he turned to Anthony.
'What about you Drax?'
At four foot ten inches Anthony was above average height for his nine years although not of stocky build. He would attain his father's five ten by the age of sixteen.
'Rugby Sir.'
'Right. First practice tomorrow afternoon on the southern rugby field' Kirby check his list again.
Teddy enrolled for cricket befitting family tradition.

Rosemary Drax was concerned at Anthony's choice of rugby as would have preferred him to enroll in cricket given it was more of a gentleman's game. She respected his decision though and they poured over several books from their meager library dealing with the game, its history and strategies. Anthony was determined to learn everything he could about rugby. By the time he went to bed Anthony decided he would be a winger, as the kudos for tries would need to be his at any cost.

Mr Craven a mathematics teacher who took in the year four groups, helped conduct rugby practice for the squads Timothy Craven looked like a rugby player, five eight, of stocky build with close-cropped hair. He didn't look like a mathematician in which he was a master.

The new rugby players merged with the older boys at the southern rugby field.

'There are fifteen new boys from year four joining us today' said Craven 'the rest opted for cricket'

A murmur of distaste rippled through the boys as cricket was viewed with disdain and those involved as lesser beings. Once in rugby you were viewed by those already there as joining the elite. Them and us competitiveness within rugby was fierce even though all were Allard family. Although initially, he was not particularly good at it, Anthony took to rugby like a duck to water and not long into the season was designated a winger. Fast and furious he took the knocks, giving as good as he got. As a strategist he didn't go unnoticed by Craven. Anthony's skill was in using the team for his own ends so was perceived as not really a team player. That all-important try and the accolades that went with it continued to be important for

Anthony. There was a cautious respect for him although the other boys sensed the underlying self-motive and were somewhat annoyed at his individuality and opportunism that frustratingly yielded results.

It was the first time that Anthony fully realised strategies could be used to fuel his insatiable ego. He needed to be appreciated and receive the recognition he deserved. He couldn't conceive that life could or should be any different. His involvement also continued in athletics much to the delight of Kirby although rugby under Mr Craven was well established as his first preference. Both gave equal time to Anthony who was aware that he had managed to use them to his advantage. His mother, on the other hand, who was always there to pander to his needs either in or out of school, followed his sporting development with fervor.

Anthony excelled in mathematics consolidating his relationship with Craven. As year four progressed, Anthony improved academically achieving the top position overall reinforced by his sporting prowess winning the respect of staff and students alike. Physically he developed into a strong well-built boy. This environment began to be consciously exploited by Anthony, his inner secret, which would establish his behaviour in all aspects throughout his life.

'Hi Anthony.' greeted Teddy as they met on their way back to the school building to await their home commutes.

'Teddy! How the devil are you? How's cricket?' Anthony was in good humour after his position in the rugby juniors had been confirmed for the third time. He wasn't really interested in Teddy.

'Going well actually. I made it to the junior eleven for the

next inter school game next weekend. You?'
'Haven't been out of the Allard junior rugby squad yet. Three games under my belt.' a wry smile wasn't missed by Teddy.
'Well done, indispensable I imagine. I still need to prove myself. Always up for a challenge though.' Teddy disclosed his shortcoming.
It was early autumn, leaves on the turn and the hint of a chill in the air. They both walked on in silence happy with their lot.
'You know, I've been meaning to ask if you would like to come over one weekend. I asked father and he had no objections. You could even stay over if you want.' proposed Teddy
Anthony was taken off guard, stopped and stared at Teddy. Never in his short life had he been ask such a thing. He was confused for a moment and thought what was in it for Teddy? What was in it for him?
'I'll ask mother and let you know tomorrow.' Teddy continued.
Rosemary Drax was delighted when Anthony told her of the offer and said he most certainly must go. She would drive him over the weekend after next and would call Mrs Matthews to confirm. Rosemary had been concerned that Anthony spent all available time with her and never preferred to play with the boys of his own age. This was a pleasant development. Had something changed?
'Well, did you ask your mother?' Anthony asked Teddy the next day.
'Mother said it would be alright to stay over after she confirms with your mother.'

'Good. That's settled then.' Anthony responded.

There was an air of comfort and ease for the people of Teddington and the boys at Allard Grammar. Each year would continue to be a seamless progression. Year five was just around the corner.

Teddington Manor sat in five acres of gardens overlooking the Thames. The boat shed on the bank was a favourite place for Teddy to hang out. Hugh Alwyn Matthews, senior partner of Matthews, Fortescue & Miller, gazed out of the bay window down the lawn, past the boat shed, over the Thames to the row of houses on the far bank without really seeing them. He drifted. Movement broke his solitude as Sophie and Teddy walked towards the house. He was very fond of them and knew they had been chatting in the boatshed loft sharing one of Sophie's cigarettes. They didn't know he knew. Sophie would go to Cambridge, as would Teddy, to study law, preferable an LLM in corporate and commercial law. Sophie would be the first female in the family to study law. He envisaged them working in Matthews, Fortescue & Miller, his company, given that Fortescue and Miller had sold their shares to Hugh before the war. Hugh had contributed his contract law skills during the war to the government. The laughter, complimenting the warm sunny late afternoon, broke his reflection. Mrs Matthews was preparing dinner.

'Hello daddy' Sophie flowed into the room.

'Hello darling'

'Teddy'

'Hello dad'

'We have been to the boat shed daddy'

'I know dear. I saw you and Teddy walking back.'

Sophie kissed her father on the cheek. He felt content in this environment. This house that had been in the family for just over a hundred years gave him much needed respite from the stress of the practice.
'How is cricket Teddy?'
'I'm in the junior eleven for the inter school game next weekend.'
'Well done, keeping the family tradition alive.'
Sophie and Teddy were comfortable with family tradition without question.
'I had a telephone call from Mrs Drax this afternoon' Mrs Matthews informed the family at dinner.
'Anthony will be over next Saturday afternoon for dinner and will stay overnight, Teddy.'
'Cricket doesn't finish until late afternoon mother' Teddy exclaimed.
'Well, you asked him over Teddy. I am sure you will be back in time dear.'
At Hugh's insistence Teddy gave them an overview of Anthony, which was when he realised he didn't really know much about him or his family even though they only lived down the road.
Saturday proved to be sunny and warm, partly cloudy, but a pleasant day when the Bentley entered the driveway to Teddington Manor. Rosemary alighted as Anthony unceremoniously stepped out of the car to be greeted by Mrs Matthews. Teddy wasn't back from cricket. Anthony gazed out the bay window near the lounge chair where Hugh Matthews usually sat, as his mother and Mrs Matthews had tea. The view was not unlike theirs at home.
At least he wouldn't be home tonight to suffer his father's

disinterest. He was annoyed that Teddy wasn't there.

His mother left and while Mrs Matthews was busy in the kitchen he wandered outside and sat on the steps leading to the expanse of lawn that ran down to the boat shed.

'Hello'

Anthony turned to see Sophie step down to sit next to him.

'Hello, who are you?'

'Sophie, Teddy's older sister.'

'I didn't know Teddy had a sister,' said a surprised Anthony 'He has never mentioned you.'

'Typical Teddy! I've been his sister all his life. He told us all about you though.'

'All good I hope.'

'Of course; would you like to see the boat shed?'

They walked in silence. Anthony had had nothing to do with girls. Apart from the boys banter at school in which he didn't indulge. From the corner of his eye he assessed this slim, slightly taller, with straight long blonde haired girl. Sophie opened the door where the pristine Gibbs of Hampton river cruiser confronted Anthony. A far cry from their deteriorating dinghy moored to a lesser jetty. He was impressed.

'What a beauty.'

'Daddy's pride and joy you know. We often go up river for a picnic, when it's sunny of course. It's a Gibbs you know. It has a Nanni twenty-horse power engine. Do you have a boat?"

Anthony was impressed.

'No.' He lied.

They moved to the side to view her in all her glory.

'Lets go up to the loft.'

She led the way up the narrow steep steps unaware of the eyes following her. Anthony hadn't given much thought to girls, definitely different. The pitch roof loft was sparsely furnished with an old sofa facing the river window.
'Come and sit here'
The sofa was old and comfortable. Anthony gazed out at the river. Sophie, three years Teddy's senior, reached under the sofa and brought out a small tin containing a pack of Woodbines and matches. She withdrew one of the cigarettes.
'Would you like one?'
'No thank you.'
Sophie lit the cigarette and sat back. Some of the boys at Allard smoked behind the cricket pavilion but he had never been interested nor invited to participate.
'Why don't you play cricket?'
'Because I play rugby.'
'I thought all boys liked cricket. Rugby is such a rough game, don't you think?'
'It can be difficult. I'm a winger so I need to get as many tries as possible.'
'Tries?'
' Take the ball through the oppositions defence and over the back line to score points.'
'Oh, the Matthews only play cricket. I play tennis at school' declared Sophie.
Anthony returned his gaze to the river and watched a motorboat move slowly past the window. They sat in silence with cigarette smoke spiraling upwards. He pledged never to smoke. He was bored.
'Hi everyone' Teddy called from the boatshed door.

'Up here' responded Sophie

Anthony rose and descended the stairs. Sophie extinguished the cigarette and followed.

'Nice boat' said Anthony to Teddy

'Yes, she's grand. Next time you come over I'll see if father will take us out.'

Teddy, still in his creams, chatted about cricket on the way back to the manor. They had been defeated by forty-three runs. Anthony couldn't see the point in discussing a loss. The Allard junior rugby team had won all of their games but Anthony said nothing.

Dinner was quite formal. Conversation centered on Mr and Mrs Matthews asking Anthony questions then lapsed into sport, otherwise, inane chatter. Formal and orderly thought Anthony. He will have his own manor one day.

❖

It was 1964. The years seemed to have passed seamlessly. Anthony and Teddy, at sixteen, were in year eleven at Allard Grammar and with one year to go before Teddy entered Cambridge. Anthony was still uncertain. His grades were impressive. Their friendship had remained conjectural and relaxed. Anthony enjoyed regular visits to Teddington Hall, which he found quiet, secluded, a peaceful escape from his somewhat overbearing mother. He integrated well with his enigmatic personality taken as well behaved and conciliatory. He ensured he didn't encroach on the Matthews family's well-established routines, responding where appropriate, making sure their entrenched attitudes, opinions and values weren't challenged. Sophie was already at Cambridge enjoying law in this most beautiful historic city, its elegant architectural, surrounded by green spaces. She enjoyed relaxing on the banks of the river Cam or socialising with her fellow students in the many bars and cafes, new experiences and people. Sophie was happy there, worked hard to exploit this opportunity for her future. Life was good. Although she thought little of Anthony he often thought of her having infrequently enjoyed her company looking forward to her home visits. Their friendship grew over the years, spending hours in conversation, exploring the workings of life and the world. They were both intellectual with surprisingly similar views, which led to a comfortable companionship.

Anthony lounged on the sofa gazing out at the Thames with its activity on this warm sunny peaceful afternoon. Teddy would be home soon from cricket. Relaxed, he drifted off.

'Hello you.'

He awoke with a start as Sophie sat herself next to him on the sofa, closer than usual. Her closeness was disquieting yet somewhat erotic, not that he hadn't thought about her sensually before. Wondering what it would be like to hold her and to kiss those inviting red lips.

'Hello to you too, I didn't expect you.'

'An unscheduled visit I'm afraid. Mother is having tea with some friends up at the house.'

She lent over and kissed him on the cheek and uncharacteristically snuggled in. Sophie had been in an unconsummated relationship for several months with one of her colleagues. Last night she decided that he would take her virginity he had stood her up at the last minute much to her chagrin. Confused, frustrated and somewhat angry she caught the train home to get away. No doubt he would call but he had to be taught that she was not to be messed with. It was all a little condescending and hurtful.

Anthony moved his arm around her, feeling her left breast pressing into the side of his chest. He was aroused. Slowly he lifted her chin, softly kissing her red inviting lips. She moved up into his arms, held his head and kissed him slowly, passionately, for what seemed an eternity.

Breathing quickened, passions rose. Sophie and Anthony caressed each other slowly, unquestionably leading to the point of no return. These two virgins made love, not frenetically but with maturity beyond their years and inexperience. Lying in each other's arms they savoured what was a close intimate sharing, beautiful and natural, devoid of awkwardness and guilt. All seemed very natural and uncomplicated with Sophie having achieved what had been denied the previous night, a pleasant life changing surprise. They had both changed in that one act and it showed as they strolled, in silence, up the large expanse of lush green lawn towards the grandeur of Teddington Manor.

'Hello there' Teddy was home 'what have you two been up to?'

It would be five years before they would next meet.

2

On a Monday morning in June, Hugh Matthews travelled by train to Waterloo Station taking a cab to the office at 28 King Street, a short walk from The East India Club where he had a private apartment taken by his father when the business was first established. Winter had been mild with a dry spring and summer was upon them. The war had been good to Hugh and the business. They managed many of the contracts for suppliers to the war effort. The relationships and contacts that had been made were impressive. Much of the business, including government contracts, from the various industries had continued after the war. Matthews, Fortescue & Miller's reputation as a firm but fair legal service was proven and strong. It would remain so as long as Hugh or his family was in charge. The numerous mediation cases during the war had established a new avenue for the company and set a model for the future of law.

Hugh entered his first floor offices. It was tight, not cramped, for the seventy-five staff but Hugh had been thinking about new premises. They had taken on many disciplines since the war with the latest being litigation, where mediation failed.

'Good morning Mr Matthews' greeted the receptionist. Miss Jackson, his personal secretary knocked on his door and entered. She had been there as long as Hugh, a much-valued person at the front of the business, vetting clients and generally coordinating the business. She was a divorcee of three years and Matthews Fortescue & Miller was her life. Long hours, committed and uncomplaining, Miss Jackson had more knowledge of the Company the he did, something he was sure of. Hugh looked at her with admiration and respect.

'Good morning Miss Jackson, what's on the agenda today?'
'Partners meeting at 10:30, two appointments this afternoon, the second with Harvey Montague from Montague Engineering due at three thirty. He has provided a briefing document.' Miss Jackson placed the file on Hugh's desk. They discussed the week's business for some time before she left to make a cup of Hugh's favourite, Darjeeling tea.

Hugh opened the folder and scanned through the few pages giving an overview of the issue concerning Harvey Montague.

Montague, a tall broad shouldered Yorkshire man, a Scotsman with the generosity missing as they say, Hugh smiled to himself. Hugh had known him for many years as a client and liked his intelligence with straight speaking, a spade's a spade, attitude.

'Mr Montague is in meeting room three Mr Matthews' said Miss Jackson 'The tea and biscuits are there.'
'Thank you Miss Jackson.'
'Afternoon Harvey' Hugh entered meeting room three.

Located in Peterborough, Montague Engineering had been an important and major engineering works during the war and since had broken into the international market. Hugh handled all of the important contracts. Harvey Montague had an expansion strategy that included acquiring various small engineering businesses dotted around the country to meet regional demand so cutting supply costs from the

Peterborough parent company. One such company, KDS Engineering, in Middlesbrough was the topic Harvey had come to discuss with Hugh.

'As you would have read in my briefing document Hugh, I have just acquired KDS Engineering Limited, a family business in Middlesbrough' Harvey explained 'the sale was a scam Hugh. I have been defrauded out of thousands and I want to take action against the perpetrators.'

'Litigation is a time consuming and difficult business Harvey. Did you do your due diligence before purchasing KDS?'

' Of course I did. For God's sake Hugh, you know better than to ask.' Harvey was annoyed.

'Well, what went wrong then?' Hugh restrained himself.

'The briefing document I left covered that Hugh.'

'In your own words Harvey.'

Montague Engineering had several small but lucrative contracts in Middlesbrough and surrounds. On analysis it would be cost effective to manufacture the products in the area under the umbrella of the Montague Engineering management and administrative services. KDS had been flagged as a potential purchase and seemingly the best option of three on offer. There was even a possibility of exporting products through Teesport, Middlebrough's well-appointed port, to international clients.

Harvey asked his finance director to carry out the initial due diligence on KDS and to this end KDS provided a comprehensive report and audit, professionally prepared by an accountancy company in London. Although Montague Engineering had some cash in the bank it was on the low side, forward contracts would easily sustain the going concern of the company in the short term, so with the proposed work from Montague Engineering it would be in good shape. The independent third party asset valuation gave good value for investment. More importantly, KDS had the equipment needed to manufacture the required products as visually verified by Harvey's finance director. There were neither outstanding creditor claims nor concerns with staffing. The valuation was higher than what Harvey had in mind and on negotiation they met at a purchase price suiting both parties. The purchase went ahead.

'What went wrong then Harvey?'

'Basically the books, valuations and audit had been cooked Hugh.'

'You missed all of this on due diligence? Were there too many assumptions on your part?' Hugh decided to play devil's advocate.

'We did everything by the book. You know very well how I am Hugh I don't make assumptions. Everything checked out over the six months it took. We were so thorough. Even our investigations in and around Middlesbrough came out positive, actually glowing. It was like a regional collusion.'

Hugh looked thoughtful for a moment.

'What was the end result for you Harvey? Where does this leave you if no action is taken?'

'I have a white elephant riddled with debt and it's doubtful if I can even manufacture what we had planned. In total, including assets, I reckon I have paid five hundred thousand pounds over net worth. The company was virtually bankrupt with assets worn out and almost useless and the owner penniless to boot. It's a disaster. We need to do something.' Harvey looked frantic and miserable.

'The problem is that if the owner is penniless, as you say, you won't get anything back even if you take action. It will cost, Harvey, so you may only compound your financial losses. These situations are never easy.'

Hugh had been down this road before and it usually ended in tears for the litigator as most times they rushed headfirst more out of anger and bruised ego.

'All right, in your own words, explain in detail what had been cooked.'

'I borrowed the full purchase amount Hugh, using collateral from the parent company plus a personal guarantee. Business is steady but cash flow tight. I have over extended for God's sake and have to go back to the bank to disclose the situation. A bloody disaster! They will most likely suspend my overdraft.'

'In you own words Harvey.' Hugh kept Harvey on track.

Harvey explained that the KDS accounts for the past five years had entered most of the long standing debts as provisions then conveniently removed the provisions from the audited accounts presented to Harvey. It was only when the sale went through that many of the creditors contacted Montague Engineering demanding payment. As far as he could tell there was, in total, £148,000 being claimed. Furthermore, the asset valuations, carried out by local third party valuers, were over inflated by at least £200,000. Several of the forward contracts had been withdrawn that led Harvey to suspect they were bogus in the first place, purely to mislead for the purpose of sale. To make matters worse, the covering audit gave the business a clean bill of health, definitely a going concern.

They discussed the details in depth before Hugh sat back and looked carefully at Harvey.

'As I said Harvey, litigation is difficult and usually more unsuccessful than not. However, there may be a case to answer here.' Hugh needed to ensure that he didn't mislead or give false hope.

'I suggest that the first step, if you wish to engage us, would be to carry out an initial assessment of the situation. I will need to work out the fee for service.'

After discussing costs, Harvey agreed to proceed to the next step and would send all documents within the next two days. Hugh ushered Harvey from the meeting room to the office entrance. They shook hands and as Harvey turned to leave.

'By the way, who carried out the audit?' Hugh asked.

'Maddison & Chapman.' Harvey descended the stairs and was gone.

Hugh stood fixed looking at the door. He felt uneasy. Maddison & Chapman he definitely knew. His father and Reginald Drax had been associated with some common projects during the war until Reginald was vaporised, poor fellow. The principal now was Henry Drax, Reginald's son and Anthony's father. Even though Anthony was Teddy's friend Hugh concluded there was no conflict even though a negative outcome for the Drax family may be difficult for them.

Matthews Fortescue & Miller received the documents from Montague Engineering in the afternoon of the second day to be reviewed by the litigation team. Hugh would personally supervise this case.

It was two weeks before the litigation team came up with its decision that there was enough evidence to proceed. Hugh didn't like this side of law, so messy and unpleasant. The only difficulty was that the owners of KDS Engineering, Keith David Simpson and his wife Katherine seemed to have disappeared. There is always the challenge of having enough defendants of means listed by the claimant in a lawsuit to ensure a reasonable chance of a successful payout including costs. Without this, to proceed would be foolish. It comes down to having a good case and certainty of payout. A claim against multi defendants would need to be approved by the court.

In its draft writ, Keith and Katherine Simpson, three valuers, two government funded organisations and auditors Maddison & Chapman were named as defendants. Rigorous review would be carried out before the writ would be issued.

❖

Keith and Katherine Simpson sat drinking their morning coffee at the kiosk on Les Palmeres beach, south of Valencia. Born in Middlesbrough, with Spanish ancestry, Keith and his wife Katherine quickly moved to Spain after the sale of their engineering business. They were never to return to England. Frequent visits to Spain over the years had enabled them to put everything in place for their permanent move to Les Palmeres well before the sale. Facing bankruptcy, a reprieve had been handed to them by Maddison & Chapman one of their creditors. Cap in hand, Keith went to London to explain to Henry Drax the almost hopeless situation the business faced. Henry, facing difficulties himself, worked with Keith to develop a strategy to facilitate the sale of KDS Engineering. Maddison & Chapman would receive their outstanding fees plus costs, doubled. A tidy sum that would settle the outstanding debts of Maddison & Chapman with the surplus transferred to Henry Drax's personal account that was also in Spain into which Henry had been siphoning money from the business for years. A tidy sum had accrued, a contingency against unforeseen developments.

Time was of the essence. Henry quickly compiled a draft audit. They shared the task to fill in the holes. Henry doctored the last five years of annual accounts to fit the audit while Keith called up 'favours' from three valuers promising an attractive success fee well above industry standards, once the sale went through. Each of the valuers were kept at arms length from each other, each thinking that they were the only one involved. Keith specified each varying value, within a workable range, so that he would write a report with the average value commensurate with the audit. The average of the values would be significantly above true value.

Keith was a well-known and respected entity in the region, although, always on the border when it came to ethics, a regional trait. He was perceived as a shrewd and firm businessman, hard working, while supporting the business community as well as having been appointed to several working committees promoting the region. His involvement as a judge for the annual business awards added further credence to his standing within the community. He was invited to and attended many black tie business functions each year, which, he didn't particularly enjoy, however, it was part of the game. One day he may need to call on support and that day had come. He carefully selected the two most naive government organisations he had a relationship with and approached them for their reference and support, on the grounds of seeking expansion funding for the business. At the thought of bolstering their own reputations they wrote detailed and glowing reports including comments on Keith's integrity and high standings in the business community. These reports would contribute significantly to the purchase of KDS Engineering by Harvey Engineering. Unbeknown to each, they would be implicated in the fraud and served a writ. The prosecutor would rigorously pursue the issue of such documents influencing greatly this obvious and serious well-orchestrated fraud. Their eagerness to support without proper due diligence would be their undoing. Thus was the nature of such regional machinations where cohorts pampered egos and reports were engineered to satisfy criteria for funding from the central government primarily to protect their own jobs rather than for the benefit of the region. A means to their own ends, above practical reality, ethics, morals and the law, so they thought. In this instance the repercussions of the successful prosecution would result in much ducking and diving, sacrificing the mandatory scapegoat but it would not stave off being put on notice for a serious breach of funding criteria, rules and regulations. Such a caution would do little to dampen the entrenched cronyism and ineffectual business outcomes they would be guilty of in the future. Regroup, rename and soldier on was the strategy.

At last all was in place and the documents were supplied to

Harvey Engineering in Peterborough. The negotiations and sale were completed within three months. With proceeds of the business and their house sale in the bank, Keith and Katherine Simpson were in Spain within three days of the receipt of funds where they would enjoy a very comfortable retirement. Valuers had been paid along with Maddison & Chapman and Henry Drax's private Spanish account received an impressive financial boost. All involved were pleased with the outcome.

Harvey picked up the telephone.

'Hello.'

'Harvey, its Hugh, I have been through the documents you sent and given the situation due consideration. Taking into account all aspects of the situation you may very well have a case with a reasonable chance of success.'

'What do you mean reasonable chance?' Harvey was suspicious of solicitors. They were always circumspect in everything except their fees. They seemed to drag out everything and inevitably a loose estimation of costs was just that, loose. In the end it always cost considerably more than you were led to believe. He had never come across a situation where costs were less than a 'loose' estimation. Fixed fees were almost impossible to achieve when engaging legal advisors. Proposed outcomes were often just as abstract.

'Well, there is clarity in that your were deceived into believing that KDS Engineering was in good condition and would be able to meet your requirements. Furthermore, there is an indication that there may have been collusion between those involved. In short, you have a case to proceed with. Now, if the court feels the same way then we stand a good chance of a decision being brought down in your favour.' While Hugh genuinely felt it was a good case he didn't favour a positive outcome for Harvey.

Harvey hated 'should', 'could' and 'stand a good chance', why couldn't they be more definite, even certain. It was so annoyingly ambiguous. But that's the law and lawyers for you, always covering their necks. No doubt there would be the usual disclaimer to sign, further removing risk from the solicitor.

'Okay, given it's a good case with a strong possibility of a favourable outcome. Who am I actually suing? The Simpsons seems to have disappeared.'

'Good point, Harvey. We will go for multiple defendants. For starters it will be the Simpsons irrespective of where they are. We will investigate their whereabouts and issue the claim. They'll be found Harvey. KDS Engineering is out, as you own it. Maddison & Chapman are still trading and probably the main perpetrator, as we confirmed they conveniently left out provisions from the original accounts lodged with Companies House in the audit. So they are next on the list then Henry Drax, personally, followed by the three independent valuers and their respective companies, as well as the two quasi government agencies. However, we may be required to go through the laborious complaints procedure against them before the court will consider any action against the government agencies. At least it will give them a fright and there will no doubt be internal head rolling.'

'Who has the money Hugh?'

'Worse case Simpsons evade any action against them, we have a strong contender in Maddison & Chapman and

Henry Drax. We may get something out of the valuers and their companies but more likely than not as they acted in good faith with much of it based on the information they were fed. They will have insurance cover though. Their company accounts show that they are small players and the individuals have limited assets. It will hurt them though. May get something but not a lot as depends on the mood of the court.'

There he goes again with the 'worse case', 'may' and 'if', Harvey mused. They are all the same, nothing definite, always covering their necks. His hatred of anything legal, especially the cost increased.

'So, its Maddison & Chapman and Henry Drax' Harvey felt despondent 'most likely for the majority of the claim then? The others may contribute or at the very least cover costs and fees.' Hugh knew what was coming next.

'Will you work on a success fee Hugh?'

'Harvey, its company policy that we don't, you know that. As always we will ensure you are briefed every step of the way and we have our in house barrister, a specialist in litigation, so that will help greatly. Before we proceed I'll submit an estimation given all goes according to plan.'

Harvey's despondency deepened to the mention of estimation. Double it and it will be somewhere near, he thought.

'Well then what makes you think Maddison & Chapman or Henry Drax have money?' Harvey was having difficulty seeing the reduced risk.

Hugh explained that they had investigated Maddison & Chapman to find it moderately healthy for a small, edging on medium company. Revenue had been consistent over the past five years due to bread and butter clients of similar size. With at least twenty percent larger but not so regular clients they have a reasonable turnover. Drax takes a handsome salary and dividend payments to maintain Westwood and keep his wife in a more than reasonable life style. However, the icing on the cake was that the company has a long-standing legally registered fixed lien over Westwood House from previous borrowings. It states that the property can be used as collateral for all Maddison & Chapman debts, even though the property is in Drax's wife name, she had signed the lien. The lien had been used for several small borrowings with all cleared except for a recent quite large borrowing with interest only payments being made. The equity in the house is more than enough to cover the claim plus Drax owns a small flat in London.

'It is this situation, Harvey, that makes the action against Maddison & Chapman and Henry Drax worth while, even attractive.'

'Assuming I go ahead with the claim what is the procedure?' Harvey understood full well what Hugh proposed but he was still nervous. Someone like Henry Drax, with his back against the wall would fight tooth and nail and was probably as slippery as a solicitor. Harvey smiled to himself.

'How do you propose we lock the assets in so they can't be sold from under us?' Harvey needed to have total confidence before agreeing to proceed.

'At the same time the claim is registered and issued, we will take out an injunction to stop the sale of Westwood House and Drax's flat.'

The two men discussed the matter at some length before Hugh invited Harvey to lunch where they went over it again. Harvey was feeling more comfortable with proceeding especially after a filet mignon and half a bottle Chateau Mouton Rothschild.

'Harvey, sleep on it and if you feel the same in the morning we'll proceed. Give me a call either way.'

The two men left the restaurant and went their separate ways.

Next morning Hugh picked up the phone.

'Very well Harvey, we'll get onto it straight away. I'll keep you fully briefed every step of the way and don't hesitate to call me anytime to discuss. Have confidence.'

Harvey never had confidence with anything to do with solicitors or the courts as it could go any way depending on the 'mood of the court', a term used by the lawyers to lay blame on someone else to cover their own incompetence. Harvey grimaced.

❖

'Is it that time already?'

Henry Drax's one bedroom London flat was small but comfortable, some ten minutes walking distance from the office. The woman in the bed was Helen Montgomery, Harvey's person assistant. Helen was nothing like Mrs Drax, fifteen years younger, with a slim body and a healthy sexual appetite. She was mature and attractive with an amiable personality. No one in the office or outside guessed that Henry and Helen had a long-standing relationship, as they were very discrete. They were friends and lovers, comfortable with each other spending as much time as possible together usually at Henry's flat from

Friday night to Monday morning. Once every two months they would catch the train to Brighton where they enjoyed being Mr and Mrs Henning at the Sea View Hotel. They discussed plans to move to Spain, once Henry retired, were they would settle. Helen was convinced by Henry that his wife would be comfortable owning Westwood House with sufficient revenue from investments which although fictitious served to placate any concerns Helen may have. A divorce was fait accompli. Henry avoided discussing Anthony of whom Helen was aware and knew he was estranged from Henry. Anthony would remain with his mother. There would be no further contact with Anthony.

'Breakfast is ready.' Henry called as Helen emerged from the bedroom in her dressing gown. They were happy with their lot.

In the office their behaviour was formal without a hint of anything but a working relationship. They were perfectionists, never wavering nor making a suspicious mistake, which not so much by design but more a reflection of the disciplined nature they both shared. Helen the archetypal spinster who was organised and well mannered with a firm but pleasant demeanor, proved to be a perfect personal assistant.

Helen left half an hour before Henry to arrive at the office precisely at 8:30 am followed by Henry who never got in before 9:00 am.

On this Monday morning Henry arrived at 9:15 am, walked through to his office, hung his coat and removed some papers from his brief case, sat down to start the days work. Miss Montgomery knocked politely and entered.

'Here is your tea Mr Drax and I have this week's meeting

schedule. Don't forget that Mr Reynolds won't be in this week due to his holidays.'

'Thank you Miss Montgomery.'

A tall man in a trench coat strode into the office unannounced.

'Excuse me, can you tell me if Mr Drax is available?'

Helen looked up a little startled.

'Have you an appointment?' Helen asked tersely. She didn't appreciate such unscheduled requests, certainly not from the likes of this man.

'No it will only take a minute.' The man stared directly at Helen.

'I am sorry, you will need to make an appointment.' Helen was rattled especially as he hadn't the decency to remove his hat.

The man looked around the office and realised that apart from the open office there was only one glassed walled office with the occupant at the desk reading a file. Without further comment he moved around Helen's desk making for the office door.

'You can't go in there without an appointment ...... '

Helen's raised voice alerted Henry who looked up to see a stranger making his way to his office with Helen in pursuit. He got up from his desk just as the man entered the office. Walking up to Henry he thrust two thick manila envelopes into Henry's chest. Henry involuntary clutched the envelopes.

'What in God's name....' Henry bellowed.

'You've been served.' the stranger said firmly, turned and left the office.

Henry Drax and Miss Montgomery stood in stunned silence

until Henry dropped the envelopes on the desk and sank into his chair, ashen-faced.

'That will be all Miss Montgomery' Henry said lamely looking at the envelopes.

'Mr Drax, I....'

' Don't worry Miss Montgomery, I don't know what this is about but I will sort it out. There must be some mistake. Close the door on your way out please.'

Miss Montgomery turned, closed the office door and entered the open office, which was in dead silence as all had witnessed the incident and were just as stunned as she was. Slowly the office regained a subdued atmosphere with an undertone of surprised murmuring. Nothing had ever happened like this before.

Helen sat at her desk looking blankly at the papers stacked neatly in front of her thinking about the intrusion. Never in all the years she had been there had anything like this happened. It was unnerving to say the least. She knew that whatever was in the envelopes on Henry's desk was serious. What did this mean for them, for her? Will their plans, their future, be shattered? No, she must stay positive, they would deal with whatever it was and move on. So near to Henry selling the business for their move to Spain to start a new life.

Henry held an envelope addressed to Maddison & Chapman staring at it while his mind dredged up the only matter it could possibly be. The other was addressed to himself. He had buried it deep but it had never totally gone away. When it surfaced from time to time he was quick to block it, to be returned to the depths of his mind. Subconsciously, he had hatched a strategy should something go wrong. Henry knew exactly what was in the envelopes.

The summons showed the list of defendants to appear before Judge Godfrey S. Forsythe who would hear the case Harvey Engineering Vs. Maddison & Chapman, Henry Drax and six other defendants. Multiple defendants had been agreed between the prosecutor, Matthews, Fortescue & Miller and the court as the argument put that all named defendants were jointly and severally liable for the same damage.

Henry felt ill after reading the document several times. He had always run a clean business although sometimes borderline. It was the impressive fee that had enticed Henry to help Keith Simpson sell KDS Engineering even though it was a basket case. The positive was that he had diverted the majority of the fee into his overseas account. Much to Henry's surprise the whole process went smoothly including the manipulation and falsification of almost everything to do with the business. He was particularly impressed by the way Keith had so readily come up with the valuations and supporting documents. The package presented to Harvey Engineering was neat, tidy and would stand up to a superficial due diligence for the purchase and by the bank that issued the mortgage. Harvey Montague was eager for the purchase to be approved so therefore accepted all on the superficial due diligence his finance director carried out on his behalf. Henry even went to great lengths to assure his bank. The accounts Maddison & Chapman had prepared for the sale of KDS Engineering were loaded with convoluted detail to disguise the removal of footnote provisions setting out the conditional payments to be made to creditors who were willing to wait until the company was in a position to make payment. These provisions were not shown in the balance sheet or the profit and loss accounts. For Harvey, the surprising aspect was that if close due diligence had been carried out these accounts would not compare with those lodged before the current year with Companies House, all showing the provisions. These changes were the only ones that Henry was guilty of but that was enough. The rest was on Keith Simpson's shoulders but Keith had fled to Spain, as Henry very well knew. Henry had a sinking feeling that he was going to take the full brunt of the claim. He needed to think quickly and be concise about his actions. The injunction on the sale of his flat he knew would mirror one on Westwood House.

'Miss Montgomery would you come into my office please. Bring your pad and pencil, thank you.'

❖

On the same day Henry had been served, all of the defendants listed were served, except for Keith Simpson. It would not be until two days before the hearing that it became clear where Keith was residing. The court would not be happy.

North East Advancement and Middlesbrough Business Promotions two government funded agencies or Quangos as they were commonly called received their summons causing a degree of panic as expected. The CEO, two board members and their legal advisor from each met the following day to discuss. Two days later all met with Hugh and Harvey at the London offices of Matthews, Fortescue & Miller. The proposal put was from the two agencies for

Harvey Engineering received two attractive business development grants conditional to the withdrawal of the agencies as defendants. Hugh and Harvey accepted the proposal with the withdrawal notice lodged to the court the following day. Harvey's confidence was buoyed by this unexpected outcome and his faith in Hugh grew.

Together, the three valuers took their summons to have them legally reviewed with the result that it was felt that they had been manipulated as each had been given different information concerning the assets they independently reviewed. Given there was no collusion nor deviation from each brief by KDS Engineering at the hearing the court ruled that there was reasonable doubt as to their contributing liability and dismissed the claim against all three.

In summing up the Honourable Godfrey S Forsythe concluded that Harvey Engineering had been wronged to the full extent of the claim against Keith Simon, Maddison & Chapman and Henry Drax. In the event of Mr Simon not being located or that Maddison & Chapman was unable to contribute to the damages then payment of the damages and all costs will be against the assets of Henry Drax with any residual against Westwood House. Furthermore Matthews, Fortescue & Miller are to be appointed as administrators for the assets of Mr Drax and Westwood House with title deeds to be surrendered immediately.

Harvey was ecstatic at the outcome, as he never imagined that it would give him full compensation but with the grants he actually got far more than expected including costs to be covered. Hugh had exceeded all expectations.

Henry's world had fallen apart and the period from the

receipt of the summons to the judges summery had taken its toll. He was exhausted and deflated to such an extent that that he found it difficult to function. Fortunately he hadn't declared his overseas account as part of his assets as it was in a trust that could not be traced.

Helen had been his stalwart during this period and had resolutely stuck to their plan that if they were faced with a worse case outcome they would leave for Spain where they could live off Henry's trust fund and her rented flat, giving them a comfortable life style. Five days later, Henry and Helen drove off the ferry onto French soil with few possessions and clothing. Helen's flat had been rented out and Henry's trust account was intact. With no goodbyes the relief was palpable.

3

Anthony had just left for Allard Grammar when the doorbell rang. Rosemary Drax tidied her hair in the hall mirror then opened the door. The tall well-dressed man was holding a manila envelope addressed to Mrs Rosemary Drax.
'Mrs Drax?'
'Yes.' She replied
He handed the envelope over which Rosemary took looking at the address.
'What is this about?' Helen asked
'Mrs Drax you've been served.' The man said politely, turned and walked towards his car.
'Could you hold on please? I don't understand.'
The man got into his car and drove slowly down the driveway towards the entrance gate.
Rosemary stared at the car.
Sitting down at the kitchen table she opened the rather formal looking envelope and took out the document. The injunction was detailed but clear in that as owner of Westwood House, until further notice she would be unable to sell, mortgage or enter into any other arrangement concerning the property. The status of the injunction would be clarified after the outcome of the court case Harvey Engineering Vs. defendants as listed including Maddison & Chapman and Henry Drax.
'Mr Drax, Mrs Drax is on the phone.'
'Put it through Miss Montgomery.' Henry was expecting the call.

'Rosemary.'

Rosemary rarely called Henry at the office or in fact spoke to him whenever he was away from Westwood which was more the case than not. Their distant relationship suited both of them in a strange way. When he was at Westwood they were cordial and pleasant which made it bearable for Henry and comfortable for Rosemary. Other than convenience and routine they had little feeling for each other and had agreed to sleep in separate rooms shortly after Anthony was born.

'I received an injunction document concerning Westwood this morning Henry. It's all very confusing and quite frightening. Why are you involved in the court case mentioned in the injunction.'

'Nothing to worry about Rosemary.' Lied Henry

'Can you mail the document to me at the office and I'll have the injunction lifted within the next week or two. All is in order and we will discuss the matter when I come down on the weekend.' Henry lied again.

Henry needed to stall Rosemary, as Westwood House was his get out of jail card and the consequences for Rosemary and Anthony were inconsequential when one was faced with self preservation.

Rosemary would neither see nor talk to Henry again as he didn't come home that weekend explaining that he had much to do concerning the rectification of the company's mistaken involvement in the Harvey Engineering matter, they weren't even a client. All would be back to normal shortly.

Actually three weeks passed before Rosemary's doorbell rang on the Saturday, early afternoon. Anthony was at rugby.

Rosemary opened the door and was surprised to see Hugh Matthews.

'Hugh, what a pleasant surprise.'

'Hello Rosemary, may I come in'

'Of course, I was just making a cup of tea, would you like a cup?'

'Yes thank you.'

Hugh sat at the kitchen table while Rosemary poured the tea. He placed the envelope he was carrying on the table.

'Have you seen or talked to Henry recently.' Hugh understood that Henry spent the majority of his time away from Westwood House with little involvement with his wife or son. Hugh had his suspicions but they were only that.

'Not recently Hugh, as he has been preoccupied with a matter that he was wrongfully implicated in and I suspect he has to stay in London until it has been resolved. Henry seems rather stressed by it all I'm afraid.'

'And Anthony?'

'He's fine. Especially when he is playing rugby, which he is doing as, we speak. He is also doing quite well at Allard and strives to achieve, he can't stand it if he's not the top in everything. You must see him when he visits Teddy.'

They discussed things in general while they drank their tea.

'What is it you wanted to see me about Hugh?' Rosemary looked at the envelope as if seeing it for the first time.

'Well it's a very delicate and serious matter Rosemary.'

Hugh carefully and tactfully explained to Rosemary point by point Maddison & Chapman's and Henry's involvement in the Harvey Engineering case. He left no stone unturned as he deemed it important that the full facts were disclosed so Rosemary who needed to understand the terrible predicament Henry had led himself and his family into. As Hugh continued Rosemary's face drained to pale grey as she stared at Hugh. Her mind started to glaze over as the full implications of what Hugh was telling her became apparent.

'Lets have another cup of tea Rosemary. I'll make it.' Hugh rose from the table to put the kettle on. He refreshed the cups and poured the tea. They sat in silence while Hugh sipped his tea. Rosemary stared at the cup.

'The most difficult aspect of all this Rosemary is that I have been ordered by the court to be the administrator for the sale of Westwood House. I can assure you though that I will make every effort to ensure that you receive as much of the proceeds as possible. Henry's flat in London will cover a reasonable amount of what is required and with your equity in Westwood House the residual should allow you to buy another smaller property for you and Anthony to live. Furthermore, I will do everything possible to support your move and you personally thereafter.'

Rosemary's world had come crashing down in a matter of two hours. She would have to leave her beloved Westwood House and God only knew where she and Anthony would end up. At least Henry would be able to support both of them if and when he found a job as there was no doubt that Maddison & Chapman would be either sold or wound up as Hugh put it.

Hugh left as Rosemary drifted to the sitting room, staring with unseeing eyes out over the lawn that led to their small jetty on the Thames. At that moment the dilapidated dinghy sank slowly to the riverbed, mooring rope attached, its gunwale barely showing above the surface, it was beyond salvage.

Anthony stood in the doorway looking at his mother staring out the window. It was a pleasant, still day with streaks of light white cloud high in the sky avoiding the light breeze that cooled the mild warmth of the distant sun. She was unmoving, statuesque as he slowly he walked toward her.

'Mother.' She failed to respond. He put his hand gently on her shoulder causing her to shudder slightly and turn, eyes downcast.

'What is it?' He asked cautiously. His mother was the only person he trusted whatever trust meant. She was neutral, the only constant in his life. Everyone else he found lacking in varying degrees. People he considered to be a means to his end so he looked for what he could gain from each, what was their usefulness, everyone slotted into his spectrum of contempt. They were either meaningless or useful to a point. He had learnt the art of projecting the necessary behaviour to elicit the response he required to give them a comfortable perception of himself. Anthony had no concept of a give and take relationship, only what was beneficial for his life.

Rosemary looked at Anthony and beckoned for him to sit.

'Anthony, there is something I must tell you.'

Rosemary relayed the explanation of recent events that Hugh had given her, step by step, detail by detail. She explained the consequences of the outcome of the court decision, which she made quite clear was the sole result of his father's actions. Westwood House is to be sold with a modest amount left that would allow her to buy a small house or flat, certainly not in Teddington. The only source of income would be from what Henry would be able to bring in from the job he would need to find as Maddison & Chapman and the London flat are to be sold. The guilt of losing Westwood House flowed over Rosemary as she talked to Anthony. She felt physically ill having let down her Westwood ancestors. How could Henry have done this to her? To abuse her trust in him was unforgivable. Rosemary made a mental note to call Henry immediately she finished with Anthony. Anthony sat passively as he listened to his mother and without flinching he took in that he would need to leave Allard Grammar. The actions of others had forced him into a situation he didn't want. But he had time on his side and in time he would make those concerned pay dearly for the inconvenience thrust upon him. In all his thinking there was no consideration of the effects upon his mother. She would be there for the next stage of his life until he could stand alone to fend for himself. Pity the Bentley had to go but he would buy his own in due course. He would need to convince Mr Matthews to assist them to buy a house and car and get the best out of a difficult situation. Void of emotion, he had no compunction in using emotional blackmail, as he knew his friendship with Teddy would come in handy one day. Sophie may also be of worth but by God he would extract his vengeance against the Matthews family one of these days. In his mind they were, or at least Mr Matthews was, one of the perpetrators of this situation, much to think about. He didn't believe in God whatsoever, finding the concept ridiculous and those who believed contemptible.

Rosemary rang Henry's office having forgot that it was Saturday, only realising when the phone went unanswered. Next she called Henry's flat, again no answer. Where is Henry, she thought, at least he could have had the decency to come down and help them through this difficult situation. Henry was egocentric at the best of times but surely he should have called her. Where was he?

It was 9:30 am on Monday morning when she called Henry's office and was answered immediately.

'Maddison & Chapman.' The clipped female voice answered.

'This is Mrs Drax, can I speak to Mr Drax please.

'Please hold Mrs Drax.' The female voice responded.

After several minutes a male voice came on the line.

'Mrs Drax, I am Leonard Hatfield of Matthews, Fortescue & Miller. I believe Mr Matthews has informed you that we have been appointed as administrators of the assets of you and your husband.' Leonard said cautiously as he was not sure how much Mrs Matthews knew.

'I have been appointed by Mr Matthews to assess and look at the options for Maddison & Chapman and this is my first day. The first two hours, so early days Mrs Drax.'

Rosemary was getting exasperated and could only focus on finding Henry.

'I appreciate that Mr Hatfield but I am trying to contact Mr Drax. Is he there?'

'Unfortunately not Mrs Drax, actually, no one has seen Mr Drax since Wednesday of last week, most strange. Incidentally his personal assistant Miss Montgomery hasn't been in either. We are trying to contact her as well.'

Rosemary barely registered what Leonard was saying. Where was Henry? Why hadn't he come home or at least called her. Rosemary's mind swirled in confusion and despair leading her to uncharacteristic floundering, how was she going to be able to resolve anything. She decided to call Hugh to seek his advice.

Hugh wasn't able to help Rosemary find Henry but pacified her explaining that it would take the rest of the week to assess what was what and work out a strategy which satisfied all parties concerned. He reassured Rosemary that he would do the best he could to ensure she received the best possible outcome financially. Hugh promised to call in next Saturday and update her on their findings.

Hugh was true to his word arriving at Westwood House at eleven am on Saturday. Anthony was playing rugby for Allard Grammar again as his mother had insisted they maintain the status quo until everything became clear.

A rather buoyant Hugh Matthews and despondent Rosemary Drax sat at the kitchen table discussing the past week's events. As always the perfect host, Rosemary provided tea and freshly baked cake that Hugh readily enjoyed as Mrs Matthews, was reluctant to have any cake in the house due to Hugh's insatiable appetite for cake. Henry had disappeared. No one could find him and he hadn't contacted the office, Hugh or obviously his wife. Hugh didn't disclose that Miss Montgomery had also disappeared and that her flat had been let. He could understand Rosemary being distraught but unfortunately, his secretly held long-standing suspicions were only compounded. Henry had absconded from his responsibilities. Hugh moved on.

'Rosemary, we must focus on your situation. The outcome of the week's assessment has been far better that I expected. We have valued Henry's flat and business, which we can sell, leaving the claim against Westwood House to be approximately thirty percent of its value, much less that fist envisaged.' Hugh was pleased with the result, a result that wasn't appreciated by Rosemary. It was unfair that she now found herself in this predicament.

'This will give you a very reasonable amount to resettle in a modest but comfortable small house or flat, leaving enough funds to see you through for years to come.'

'Surely, Henry will be able to support us when he has a new position.' Rosemary hadn't considered that it could be any other way.

Hugh had to spell it out to bring Rosemary back to reality.

'Rosemary, until we can locate Henry or he contacts you we must plan for your and Anthony's future. If something has happened to Henry you will be on your own.

Deep down, Rosemary knew something was amiss but until now she had suppressed such a thought. It would be impossible to conceive that Henry would abandon them.

It took three months for Henry's flat to be sold, Matthews, Fortescue & Miller bought Maddison & Chapman and a buyer for Westwood House had been found. Hugh helped Rosemary buy a small semi detached property in Hounslow.

As the Bentley drove slowly towards the entrance gates for the last time Anthony looked back at Allard Grammar with its early eighteen-century ivy cloaked Georgian buildings.

He had become attached to Allard Grammar from a functional aspect, nothing more. It was an environment in which he had developed, unencumbered, into an educated self-assured person. He didn't tolerate the other boys very well or they him, never including him in their inner sanctum. Not that it bothered Anthony. There was no real emotional attachment to Allard Grammar. Teddy had been minimally useful although the friendship was one sided. Never seeing Teddy or Allard again was not a problem. He loathed his father, the Matthews family and all those involved in the demise of his privileged life. Retribution would eventually be dealt upon those responsible. For now he would need to move on. Anthony, buried in thought, looked out the widow of the Bentley with unseeing eyes. It would be the last time either of them would ride in the Bentley.

❖

Anthony attended Mansfield School on the recommendation of Mr Scott. Both Rupert Scott and Alan Kirby had submitted glowing reports in support that added to his positive academic record. Both were surprised at the circumstances causing Anthony to leave Allard Grammar, feeling sorry for Mrs Drax who broke down during her explanation of the circumstances. Neither were overly concerned that Anthony wouldn't succeed or be missed by the other students. No, they hadn't had any contact with Mr Drax.

Mansfield School was state funded so there were no fees. The students were quite different to Allard Grammar but this didn't worry Anthony who squirrelled himself away to focus on his studies. Once having left Allard he subconsciously erased everything about its culture and activities. It was as if it didn't exist, as though he hadn't attended. Rugby and visits to see the Matthews ceased. Anthony made no friends at Mansfield and at the end of the year he graduated top of the school.

'Hello Mrs Drax, Anthony.' It was the first visit Hugh had made although he had called Mrs Drax several times during the year for no particular reason. Hugh felt somewhat responsible to ensure Rosemary was coping under the circumstances although for what reason he was not sure. Probably because of the Matthews and Westwood's historical relationship. Henry had not resurfaced and it seemed certain that wherever he was his personal assistant was with him. He had never discussed such things with Rosemary. Some things are better unsaid.

'Hello Hugh, so nice to see you after all this time.' Rosemary smiled. She did like Hugh and in no way saw him responsible for what Henry had wrought upon his family. His concern gave her comfort and some sense of security although she hadn't contacted him since leaving Westwood House. Nevertheless he had supported her.

Anthony did not respond and sat in unsmiling silence looking directly at Mr Matthews. Unlike his mother, Anthony detested Hugh Matthews and his family as in his eyes they were the very reason he and his mother were in this situation.

'Actually, I have come to talk to Anthony, to offer a proposition for his future.' Hugh looked to Anthony and wondered if he was doing the right thing. He had never really warmed to this serious young man who had befriended his son Teddy. There was an uneasy feeling that there was a dark side to Anthony's personality not being sure how deep it went but whatever it was his intuition told him to be wary.

Hugh addressed Anthony.

'How are you doing this year at Mansfield School Anthony?'

'Well enough Mr Matthews.' What concern is it of yours Anthony thought?

'Do you have any thoughts as to what you want do when you graduate?'

'I am weighing up my options but focussing mainly on getting through this year.' He wasn't about to discuss his thoughts or plans with the perpetrator of his misfortune.

'I understand. All the same, I would like to make you an offer. There is an accountancy apprenticeship going at Maddison & Chapman starting February next year. I have discussed the possibility with Mr Larsson, the business manager and he has agreed to give you consideration conditional on your end of year academic results. What do you think?'

Rosemary paled at the mention of Maddison & Chapman, although she knew Matthews, Fortescue & Miller had bought the company for a fair market value, it was still raw.

Anthony remained steadfastly fixed on Hugh controlling the urge to strike out at his conceited offer. How dare he, this condescending arrogant bastard, after he had profited on the failings of his father, virtually stealing their only source of income ruining any chance of a reasonable future. It was at that precise moment he decided he would, somehow, make the Matthews family pay. It would be his mission. Anthony was unable to conceive that there may have been any care, concern, good will or acts of kindness from Mr Matthews. He would need to think carefully.

'That is definitely an option Mr Matthews. Do you mind if I give it some thought and discuss it with mother?'

Hugh had seen the flash of darkness in Anthony's eyes, which unnerved him further but he realised he was doing this more for Rosemary than Anthony. He realised that the basis of the offer was more guilt than responsibility.

'Of course Anthony, I'll leave it with you and if you are interested we can make the arrangements. If it would help I can ask Mr Larsson to discuss the position with you. Take your time and all the best for your exams.'

Anthony didn't respond. Rosemary had composed herself.

'Oh, Hugh, thank you so much your kind offer as I'm sure it will be a very good opportunity for Anthony. It's so very kind of you to think about his welfare.' Anthony thought his mother was too appreciative that would no doubt be interpreted by Mr Matthews as just that. Why would she say such a thing?

Mr Matthews and his mother walked out to the front door where they stood for several minutes in quiet conversation that he was unable to hear.

The rest of the year went quickly, with exams and graduation out of the way, Anthony found Christmas upon him. He had discussed the proposal from Mr Matthews with his mother who had no other opinion other than that he should accept without hesitation.

Anthony had already come to the conclusion that he would accept the proposal, as it would best serve his purpose. A qualification in accounting would be helpful in taking him into the business world where he had no doubt he would be successful in building a wealthy future by whatever means.

4

'Welcome to Maddison & Chapman Anthony,' said Harald Larsson as he studied Anthony's rather impressive academic record. Harald was tall, pale and thin, made to look more serious by the thin silver framed glasses perched on his nose. Anthony learnt he was a procedures manager. A stickler for perfection and timing that both was appreciated by his clients but frustrated the staff. The staff found him difficult and void of humour making working in the office a lacklustre and boring task with little room for banter or laughter. Consequently, the company hadn't flourished. It was stagnant although a profitable business having not grown since Henry Drax had been ousted. Nothing was ever said to Anthony about his father; in fact, no reference was made in the four years he spent there.

'Thank you Mr Larsson.' Anthony stood in front of Larsson's desk in his pin stripped suit, white shirt and dark blue tie. He held his five foot ten inches with confidence, well dressed and looking quite dashing compared to the rest of the male office staff. He had developed into an unconventionally good-looking young man who had attracted side-glances from the receptionist, Larsson's secretary and the other two women in the office who were accountants. Nothing like new blood to breathe life into a staid office environment, the women at least thought, otherwise all else was colourless, dull and boring.

'The apprenticeship programme we have will give you an ACA qualification in three years all going well. You will then be able to become a member of the ICAEAW and after ten years you will be able to apply for the FCA. Miss Banks, who has been with us for about five years, will be your coordinator and mentor. I will introduce you and she will take it from there.' Larsson rose and walked out into the open office with Anthony following.

'Miss Banks, this is Anthony Drax our new apprentice whom we discussed. I'll leave him in your capable hands.' Larsson turned hack to his office.

'Hello Anthony.' The petite twenty eight year old, five foot five slim woman stood to greet Anthony; he noticed her business complimented her impressive shape. She broke into a welcoming smile as they shook hands. Definitely an attractive woman thought Anthony and an accountant at that.

'Please sit down Anthony.' He did what he was told sitting confidently facing Miss Banks across her desk.

'Thank you Miss Banks.'

'Call me Julie as we are going to be spending a lot of time together.' Anthony smiled to himself. At least he had an interesting mentor, a means to his end.

'First things first.' She placed a manila folder in front of Anthony. 'Here is your apprenticeship programme or curriculum for the next three years. I suggest that you read through it to get a grasp of what your in for. Your desk is over there by the bookshelf. Once you've been through the folder we'll get started.'

Anthony, sat at his desk looked around the office that he guessed hadn't changed since the war, certainly not since his father left. So this is where his estranged father had spent much of his life and his father before him. The walnut panelled walls, high white ornate ceiling, oak floor with the ordered arrangement of desks and filing cabinets, he guessed, were still in the same position from when they were installed. Light flooded in from the cathedral like arched windows overlooking the street below. Telephones rang out from time to time as the studious staff buried their heads in spread sheets and reports from various clients.

The programme didn't seem daunting and with concentration Anthony decided he would allow two years to complete the course and qualify. If Larsson thought he was going to spent ten or eleven years in this mausoleum he was very much mistaken. He was in a hurry.

First impressions were positive, a pleasant young man thought Julie as she gazed over at Anthony. There was something about him, an energy and attitude the others didn't have. He seemed older than his years with a seriousness and drive she had not encountered before in one so young. She was not sure that he was accountant material although he seemed focussed on this career path. What had attracted him to this career path she wondered. Larsson had briefed her on the Drax scandal and she pledged not to discuss or mention such matters with Anthony or any of the staff even though they were well aware of past events. Personally, he was well mannered and strangely attractive with a maturity that bridged their ten-year age gap. Time would tell.

Although he despised Hugh Matthews and Maddison & Chapman, Anthony excelled in the first year due to his well-honed mathematical skills, a photographic memory and instant recall. He learnt quickly, absorbing all put before him, allowing him to easily complete the first one and a half years of his apprenticeship in the first year. Larsson was impressed and Julie found it exciting to be working with him. The others were envious, even jealous of his abilities. In return Anthony used everyone to achieve without forming any relationships or fraternising except with Julie. It was a game to Anthony who was well aware of the underlying sentiments that gave him a macabre pleasure. By design, Anthony and Julie grew close over time with Anthony realising very early on that it would pay dividends to keep in with her as she proved an asset going out of her way to support him.

Seven months into his apprenticeship he decided to approach Julie with defined intent telling her the commute between Hounslow and London was tedious and tiring. He discussed his 'thoughts' with Julie one Friday afternoon as they were leaving for the weekend.

'The problem is travelling consumes so much time so I've been thinking about staying in London during the week. Do you have any suggestions?'

'I'll give it some thought. Lets discuss it further on Monday.' Julie lived in a small two bedroom Kensington flat owned by her parents who used it when they visited London from their country house near Winchester. However, when her father bought, on retirement, a thirty-five foot yacht moored in Portsmouth the London trips ceased and Julie had permanency.

'I have a two bedroom flat Anthony and as you are only looking to stay during the week your welcome to stay with me.' Julie had given the matter cursory consideration over the weekend with the conclusion that it would be convenient for Anthony and a minor inconvenience for her. She would also be able to further support his studies and learning as well.

'Thank you Julie, that would definitely be convenient.' Anthony had planned this carefully waiting for the opportunity. He had been grooming Julie with this outcome set firmly in his sights including offering a nominal rent that she with good will refused. Her mentoring and having an ally within Maddison & Chapman was part of his plan. Anthony had manipulated his way not only into Julie's office life but also into her private life that would be to his short-term benefit. He was satisfied that all was going to plan.

The one thing he had learnt from personal experience was that when someone was in a difficult situation they were vulnerable and primed to be exploited as had happened to his mother with devastating effects for her and Anthony although much to the gain of others. Those who gained from his mother's personal and financial ruin were people such as his father who had escaped responsibilities for his actions to live a comfortable life with his secretary in Spain and Keith Simon who also settled in Spain on the spoils from the fraudulent sale of KDS Engineering. Hugh Matthews who bought Maddison & Chapman at what Anthony thought must have been a fire sale price as well as taking the breath-taking fees from the Harvey Engineering Vs KDS Engineering case and Harvey Montague who had succeeded in obtaining KDS Engineering at a final undervalue price being finance by the bank. So, in effect Harvey Montague had added substantial value to his company without spending a great deal. It would be this lesson that Anthony would remember and base his future on. Make money from exploiting the vulnerable and finance everything by using other people's money. This dictum had been burnt into Anthony's DNA, he would fiercely live by it to exact punishment on those who had wronged him and anyone else he so chose. Ingratiate one's self with the victim, manipulate their circumstances and position them for the kill. Take the spoils and move on. This formula was simple for Anthony. It would be his game, his mantra. His narcissistic personality disorder had been with him forever, however it was the outcome of the actions of his father and Hugh Matthews that finally triggered his psychopathy. The charming Anthony was devoid of conscience and empathy even for his mother.

Julie found having Anthony live with her during the week comfortable. He was clean, tidy and considerate, although somewhat emotionally guarded. Initially, she was not sure what it was but there was something concerning him that she couldn't put her finger on and eventually dismissed it as youth, giving it no further thought.

'The office pre-Christmas party is on the week after next Anthony, are you coming?'

'I don't think so Julie.' Anthony had not attended any of the office functions nor became involved with the Friday drinks down at the White Horse after work. As a quiet reserved junior member the other staff didn't give it much thought.

'Anthony, you have been here for nearly a year now, so I think it would be good for you to at least join in with the Christmas celebrations. You don't have to drink.'

'I don't drink.' Anthony retorted.

The last thing Anthony wanted to do was to go to some stuffy Christmas works party with people he had no interest in. What was in it for him? Although he was beginning to think that it may be worthwhile to keep Julie on side and it may win him some points with Larsson. Maybe.

'Why don't you sleep on it and see how you feel about it tomorrow.' She touched his arm gently. Julie didn't want to push it but felt it would be good for him both career wise and socially. He was such a recluse, she mistakenly thought. Anyhow it would be nice to have him accompany her. Julie felt close to Anthony and enjoyed his company. Her past relationships never went anywhere as they all lacked that element of excitement she sought in a man. They were too formal and boring, no adventure in any of them, usually wanting commitment with the narrow path to marriage and thereafter. None of them had come close to the mysterious Anthony Drax with his intellect, physical strength and good looks. The age gap didn't worry her. She had often thought what it would be like to make love with Anthony, dismissing it as fantasy. She worked in the wrong environment to find her adventurer. Anyhow, Julie wasn't ready to be tied down just at the moment.

The warmth of Julie's touch was electric, immediately igniting his regular carnal thoughts he had developed around Julie. She wore her pyjamas and dressing gown at breakfast each morning but just her bathrobe from the bathroom to her bedroom in the evenings. He had to admit to himself it was very erotic. Anthony didn't have a bathrobe so wrapped a towel around himself without covering his upper body. Glances from Julie didn't go unnoticed. At the right time he thought. He had had several weekend girlfriends who served the purpose of giving him the relief he desired. They were kept at arms length until eventually he tired of them. Emotional commitment was foreign to Anthony, which contradicted his contrived charming and thoughtful front, very much a learnt behaviour that was successful in achieving his goals. When infrequently out with others his manly and courteous behaviour to all enhanced his approval even though he didn't drink. People liked him. He was bored by the somewhat juvenile behaviour of his own age group so he tended to be an infrequent attendee at parties preferring to spend time alone with the girl of the moment undisturbed. None of them could be compared to the first time with Sophie though.

'I think you are right Julie, so it's on for the Christmas dinner. Actually I am looking forward to it' he lied 'I'll stay over on the Friday night if its alright by you.'

'Fine. By the way, I am always right,' laughed Julie with unmistakable joy showing through her smile.

'You owe me one though' Anthony teased.

'I don't think so as it's you who owes me. As your mentor I know what's best for you. Back to work Mr' Julie played with him.

The work level at Maddison & Chapman was constant with spikes of overload when dealing with periods when end of year accounts came together. It was still run on traditional lines being adverse to modernising management and procedures. It was worse when it came to technology that not only frustrated Anthony but also everyone else. Larsson was of the opinion that if it wasn't broke don't fix it, an adage that contributed to his and the company's stagnation. As long as it was making a profit Hugh Matthews was happy. Larsson's buffer was that he was Hugh's friend.

It had been a long year although fruitful for Anthony and Julie with much more accomplished than they had both had envisaged. Julie had kept ahead of her workload while mentoring Anthony as recognised by the generous bonus she received on the morning of the Christmas party. Apprentices didn't receive bonuses.

The office closed at two pm on the day of the Christmas dinner as it had always been since the business was established. Julie and Anthony made their way back to her flat to freshen up and dress for dinner. Bathed and dressed, Anthony sat in the lounge reading the weekend Financial Times Julie brought back every Friday and was immersed in the current mergers and takeovers when Julie came in dressed in a black strapless sequinned evening gown. Anthony looked up then stood looking straight at Julie.

'That is a beautiful dress Julie. You look stunning.'

'You look very smart yourself Anthony.' Julie thought he looked more than smart and moved over by his side. He smelt clean and manly with his musky aftershave adding to the effect. No other man she had been with had taken the care to be so well groomed she thought.

Julie's perfume was subtle and effective. He could feel her fresh warmth. Placing her hand in the crook of his arm he said

'Shall we?'

They walked in silence enjoying each other's company for different reasons.

The Fox & Hound had been booked as it was more up market than the White Swan, with its clean well-appointed dining room and bar area befitting an end of year celebration for his staff thought Larsson. Apart from the annual bonus it was tradition for the company to cover the costs of pre-dinner drinks at the bar, dinner with drinks with the staff responsible for after dinner drinks. Larsson frowned on excessive drinking or drunkenness although it had become more frequent in recent times. Larsson always left shortly after the dinner to the appreciation of the staff. Two bottles of champagne were provided specifically for the four female staff members. Men drank pints of beer, before, during and after dinner. There had been no call for wine to be served.

Julie and Anthony entered the Fox & Hound making their way to the section of bar where their colleagues were standing in groups, drinks in hand, laughing and talking over each other about work as Anthony suspected. They had nothing else in common to talk about.

'I'm just going to chat to the girls,' Julie whispered to Anthony 'I'll see you shortly at dinner, we are sitting together.' Her warm smile reassured Anthony that all might not be lost. Anthony strolled over to the men at the bar, standing on the fringe of the group. Nobody took any notice of him. Listening to the inane prattle Anthony's mind wandered to other thoughts as to whether or not he had made the right decision. A tap on the shoulder brought him back to reality.

'Here young fellow get this down you. It'll make the conversation more bearable.' Larsson passed Anthony a pint of bitter.

'Thank you Mr Larsson.' Anthony reluctantly took the pint.

'I was pleased with our annual discussion last week Drax. You have certainly stepped up to the mark. Actually you are a first for the company, achieving such progress in your first year. Well done again Drax.'

'I appreciate your comments and support Mr Larsson and hope to be able to keep up the momentum next year.'

'Actually there was something I was going to discuss with you, now is as good a time as any,' Larsson looked thoughtful.

'You are aware that part of my role is to proof read the final client accounts from the staff before they are issued to the client for sign off then lodged with Companies House. Often, oversights and mistakes are made which need to be rectified. Would you be interested in helping me out as part of your experience by proofing some of these accounts?' Larsson look directly at Anthony and he at Larsson.

'I would be pleased to Mr Larsson,' responded Anthony without flinching or smiling. Build confidence Anthony thought.

'Jolly good Drax. I thought you may rise to the challenge,' Larsson looked pleased with himself.

'Time for dinner Mr Drax.' Julie said as she approached holding a flute of champagne.

Julie led the way into the dining room and directed Anthony to two seats. As they sat Anthony placed his full pint in front of him.

'Thought you didn't drink,' smiled Julie

'A present from Larsson,' Anthony responded.

'Well you had better do the right thing then if you want to keep in with the boss,' she laughed.

They were very much aware of the closeness and made a noticeable couple in a group who had not bothered to make the effort to freshen up before an early start at the bar. Some were already well on the way.

Dinner was surprisingly pleasant with good food and conversation although Anthony participated little. He clinically observed those around him assessing each one, coming to the conclusion that he would serve his time at Maddison & Chapman then move on to better opportunities. No one here was in a position to be of any use once he left except the company itself. What for he wasn't sure.

The evening was slightly marred by a rowdy bunch at the end of the table that settled after a stern word from Mr Larsson. Anthony had finished his pint by the end of the meal finding it refreshing and relaxing. The alcohol had some enjoyable effect. Julie had several flutes of champagne becoming bright and chirpy with the odd giggle now and then much to the amusement of Anthony.

True to protocol, Mr Larsson left shortly after they had adjourned to the bar making his goodbyes with much hand shaking and back slapping. The drinks had obviously relaxed everyone, breaking the working relationships for this one night only. Julie talked Anthony into one more pint and another champagne for herself. Forty minutes later they decided to leave without too many goodbyes before they exited by the side door. No one had given them any thought before or after they left, as it had never been disclosed that Anthony was boarding at Julie's flat during the week. They had deprived the office of information that would have occupied the gossipers for the duration.

The cold air hit them both as they came out of the warm and stuffy pub with the effect being noticeable on Julie. Anthony steadied Julie by putting his arm around her shoulders as they walked into the night. She snuggled in Anthony enjoying the contact with something stirring within her. It had been along time since she had been in close company of a man. Julie chatted and laughed all of the way back to her flat with Anthony saying little while savouring the warmth of her body and touch of her softness.

'I definitely need a cup of tea,' Julie exclaimed as they entered the warm cosy flat.

'Me too, I'll get it.' Anthony moved to the kitchen.

'Just going to change.' Julie called as the kettle started to hiss.

'Don't be long Miss Banks.'

Anthony sat on the sofa having removed his coat, tie and shoes, tea made by the time Julie emerged in her pyjamas and dressing gown. She sat next to Anthony.

'This tea is yummy.' Julie slurped which she had never done before. The tea did little to stem the effects of the alcohol. She slumped against Anthony unashamedly enjoying the closeness, throwing caution to the wind she snuggled in. Anthony placed his arm lightly around her shoulders lifting her face up to his. He kissed her delicately savouring the sweet taste and eagerness to which she responded. Not yet my lovely he thought as he lifted her unprotesting body, carrying her into the bedroom, removed her dressing gown and placed her under the covers. Anthony removed his clothes and slid in next to her. They embraced softly as he felt her urgent breathing on his neck but he didn't respond except for placing his hand under her pyjama top slowly massaging her back until she settled, drifting into a deep peaceful slumber.

Julie dreamed she was experiencing the most sensational pleasure slowly building as her body tingled with desire. It had been so long. Her body moved rhythmically to the warm sensation as her realisation came into focus that he was spooned against her moving with her rhythm as one between her legs, his hardness rubbing against her outer body. Julie moved forward placing her hand to guide him into her, slowly, gently he entered and soon she gasped as her climax hit in waves of ecstasy rolling over and over into the mist of relief and relaxation.

'I need to go to the toilet.' Julie needed a pee.

'For God's sake, I haven't finished yet!'

'I know, don't go anywhere I'll be back before you know it.'

They made love into the early hours of the morning falling into exhausted sleep until well into mid Saturday morning.

'How about some breakfast?' Anthony asked as he slid out of bed as Julie admired his slim muscular body. The only cover he could find was Julie's dressing gown. She laughed.

'Well, showing your true colours I see.'

'I'll true colour you woman. Wait there. I'll bring breakfast to have in bed.'

'Sounds heavenly.' Julie stretched and turned snuggling into the blankets dozing while Anthony busied himself in the kitchen.

'Here we are.' Anthony said as he placed the tray of toast and tea on the bed before disrobing and slipping in beside Julie.

'You've excelled yourself, toast and tea! I see you need some mentoring in the kitchen as well.'

'What about the cheese and tomato?'

Saturday was a perfect day to stay indoors rather than face the wet blustery weather that wasn't forecast. They spent the day in bed exploring the delights of this newfound relationship Julie had previously thought about but hadn't really expected. He was very different from the awkward insensitive inexperienced lovers she had before. She wondered but would never ask. Anthony had expected it and only had to wait for the opportunity. She would serve his purpose for the duration of his time at Maddison & Chapman. He got his bonus after all.

The weather cleared on Sunday so they walked to Café la Fleur for coffee and croissants. Later they wandered around Holland Park with Julie being surprised that Anthony was averse to holding hands or showing any sign of emotion. So matter of fact about everything that it annoyed her somewhat.

Later that evening Anthony convinced Julie that due to their work situation it would be better if they kept the mentor relationship at work.

'We need to be professional about this.' He convinced her. Unconsciously he had managed to replicate his father's situation at Maddison & Chapman.

Anthony never did stay the weekend again. Julie was locked in and grew to regret their relationship that eventually sent her into depression robbing her joyous nature and pleasant personality. So good was the ruse, colleagues noticed her change but were confused as to why.

The second year of his apprenticeship started better than the first as he had acquired so much knowledge previously it wouldn't be a surprise to all when he would complete the three year course in record time.

❖

'Anthony, I would like you to spend the next week digging out some files from the archives for me and check on the information for the Internal Revenue who are querying past returns by some of our clients.' Mr Larsson handed the manila folder to Anthony. Anthony placed it on the desk without opening it.

'I have spoken to Miss Banks and she is in agreement so you can start immediately.'

It was May and well into spring with days warmer, trees well foliaged and people generally more cheerful. Anthony and Julie had settled into a routine with Anthony returning home on weekends. Julie missed him but wouldn't admit that she loved him although within her heart she knew she did and hated herself for it. It was a futile relationship that taxed them both. They still slept together but not as regularly, determined solely by Anthony wants or needs, whatever it was. For Anthony, Julie was a convenience. He did dabble in the odd affair on weekends without comprehension of wrongdoing, guilt or unfaithfulness to Julie. There was no relationship with Julie. He knew his charm would get him what he wanted without having to commit to anyone at anytime, both in personal matters and business.

Unbeknown to Mr Larsson or Anthony, Anthony had been placed in a position that would disclose information of devastating outcome for Hugh Matthews and Maddison & Chapman. It would also give Anthony his first real sense of power and control that he would exploit to its fullest with unimagined rewards.

All went well with the archive task with Anthony coming up with the information required by Mr Larsson who was pleased with the way Anthony approached his tasks with diligence. He was a smart lad and would go along way thought Mr Larsson not for the first time.

It was on the second to last day when Anthony searching for a particular file lifted an archive box noticing the one underneath was bound with a red confidential sticker prominently displayed on the lid. He slid it out turning it on its side to read the contents label. Harvey Engineering Vs. Maddison & Chapman jumped out at him.

In the seclusion of the archives room he removed the bonds to leaf through the hanging files one by one. Nothing seemed to be amiss as it was all fairly mundane and innocuous. It was only when he was replacing the last file that he noticed underneath the hanging files on the floor of the box an unmarked A4 envelope, which he removed. It was sealed. He decided it was too risky to see what was inside so he later secreted it inside his briefcase to take home where he would be able to inspect the contents without interference.

'Any chance of staying over the weekend?' It was Thursday evening and Julie already knew the answer.

'I thought we could spend some time together. Have dinner, see a film or just walk in the park.' Julie said with hopelessness showing through. This was the first week they hadn't made love. She was frightened that she would lose him. In a way she almost hoped he would leave her to put her out of this misery. Damn him she thought. He is really so callous while being so very charming. He never did anything wrong as far as treating her in a very proper manner at all times. Never got angry, yelled or caused her angst. There was an underlying coldness though with everything on his terms. She knew there would never be commitment.

'You know I go home on weekends, we have discussed this before.' Anthony smiled as he took her into his arms to kiss her softly, holding her gently. He never explained why or made excuses. It never occurred to him to do so. He couldn't even conceive that Julie would want more from this relationship.

By the end of the weekend Anthony had been through the contents of the envelope after steaming it open. The documents were so condemning that he was amazed they had been left at the bottom of the archives box where anyone could have happened across them, a mistake that would cost some dearly.

The document that had the most impact was an agreement between Hugh Matthews, Harvey Montague and Henry Drax where the parties agreed to an arrangement that would see that Henry Drax would not contest the claim against Maddison & Chapman or himself by Harvey Engineering. Further on it was agreed that Henry Drax would not contest the purchase of Maddison & Chapman by Matthews, Fortescue & Miller. Actually, Harvey Drax would not contest anything. In consideration Henry Drax would be free to abscond to Spain to live a new and free life with his secretary and keep his off shore account. Furthermore, quarterly payments would be made to Henry's account over the following ten years. Hugh gave an undertaking that he would ensure Rosemary Drax would be looked after. Nothing would be disclosed.

Other documents, memos and letters made it clear that Henry had met, well before the claim was lodged, with Hugh and disclosed all, seeking a resolution. Hugh had convinced Harvey to enter into the deal thus tying him in by making him sign the agreement. The whole thing had been orchestrated in the most corrupt manner with a potentially catastrophic outcome for the three signatories if it ever became known what they had concocted. They had perverted the course of justice, defrauding the court, which would be seen as a most heinous crime by any judge. Hugh Matthews had recognised this at the time and suspected that he would rue the day he signed.

On the Sunday afternoon Anthony took the documents to the local library and carefully photocopied each page four times. He replaced the originals with copies into the envelope and resealed it to be replaced in the archives. The originals were safely store in a safe deposit box he arranged at Barclays bank the following week, keeping the other two copies safely hidden at his mothers house. Anthony would have no compunction in blackmailing Hugh Matthews and Harvey Montague. He would wait to deal with his father.

On Monday evening Anthony mad love to Julie as soon as they arrived at her flat. It was urgent and fierce, almost brutal, leaving them exhausted and satiated.

'Well, what was that all about?' Julie looked fondly at Anthony.

He smiled warmly and kissed her softly. God, I love him so much Julie thought snuggling into his embrace.

'I was looking forward to seeing you,' lied Anthony 'also had a quiet weekend that gave me time to think about my future. I think it's going to turn out much better than I thought.'

It's going to turn out much better for both of us Julie mistakenly thought. If only he would stay some weekends. Perhaps it will change once he's qualified and settles into a secure position at Maddison & Chapman with prospects of advancement, even a senior position. The thought excited her. Maybe all is not lost Julie pondered as they ate a late dinner. They made love every night that week but much to Julie's disappointment, Anthony returned home on Friday.

It was November when Anthony made his move. The autumn nights were drawing in with trees being denuded at an alarming rate due to the cold creeping in at every opportunity and the battering winds.

Hugh answered the door on the Sunday afternoon and was surprised to see Anthony Drax.

'Anthony, come in out of the cold.' Hugh ushered him into the sitting room where he used to watch Anthony and Teddy coming back from the boatshed.

'What brings you here?' Hugh noticed that Anthony was well dressed in a dark suit, white shirt, tie and smart overcoat. He was a strikingly good-looking fellow, far more mature than his years, Hugh thought. Very much the businessman, Hugh observed, who by all accounts was doing exceptionally well at Maddison & Chapman, according to Larsson. He had come along way since his time at Allard Grammar.

'As you know I will have completed my three year apprenticeship by the end of this year and would like to stay on Maddison & Chapman to gain further experience.'

'Your performance is commendable Anthony, to say the least. I am sure Mr Larsson will have no problem in having you as part of his team. In fact I know he won't.' Hugh and Larsson had already discussed Anthony's future.

'Actually there is more to it than that Mr Matthews.' Anthony let the word sink in.

Hugh looked blankly at Anthony.

'In January next year I will be appointed to a senior position with salary to match. I will also be appointed as a director on the Board with a fixed annual bonus. Furthermore, I will be given the sole responsibility for the Harvey Engineering account.'

Bloody presumptuous thought Hugh. Downright rude, the arrogant little sod. Hugh's dander was up.

'Now listen here Anthony. It doesn't work like that. You will be given the position and salary befitting your experience. If you perform you will have the opportunity to work your way up the ranks. You aren't in a position to dictate what you will or won't have,' snapped Hugh. He was furious.

Anthony sat calmly looking at Hugh, infuriating him further.

'Also you will gift me fifty percent of the equity in Maddison & Chapman. We will be equal partners.' Anthony didn't shift his gaze ' You are not in a position to dictate what you will or won't do.' Anthony said calmly.

'Who in the hell do you think you are?' Hugh snarled 'you have just jeopardised any chance of a position or future with the company. As of now you are finished, do you hear? What makes you think you have any right to anything you arrogant little sod.' Hugh spat the words at Anthony as his blood pressure increased to redden his face. Doesn't he know who he talking to, bugger him.

Anthony placed the envelope in front of Hugh and sat back down. The slight smirk on Anthony's lips slightly unnerved Hugh.

As Hugh leafed through the contents he paled, anger turning to confusion and disbelief. Where did Anthony get these copies? He had locked the originals in his private safe before returning the archive box to Maddison & Chapman.

'Excuse me.' Hugh rose and walked out of the room. The safe was located in the master bedroom behind a copy of The Cafe Terrace on the Place du Forum. He did admire Van Gogh but had no originals of his or any one else's work. He reached to the back of the safe where the documents we hidden behind a false panel. The plain envelope was still sealed. He opened it and removed the papers. He starred in disbelief as he leafed through them. With a sickening feeling he realised that these were not the documents he thought were there. How had he got it so wrong, an absolute disaster?

'Where did you get those documents from?' asked Hugh as he strode back into the sitting room. His tone measured.

'They were in an archive box at the office.' Anthony was annoyingly relaxed. 'When I copied the documents I replaced the originals back in the archive box' he lied 'They are still there.'

'Blackmail is a serious offence Anthony. You would do well to think carefully about what you are doing.' Hugh lowered his gaze and thought for a moment.

Anthony's gaze didn't waver.

'I'll tell you what's going happen. I will collect the documents from Maddison & Chapman and you will return all copies you have made. In compensation, I will ensure that you receive an appropriate position with a pay rise commensurate and there will be an understanding between us that all will be forgotten about the matter. No one is going to benefit in the long term if you go down the road you are taking.' Hugh was satisfied that Anthony would see the error of his ways.

Anthony rose.

'You are in a very difficult position Hugh as the public prosecutor because the Court would be less than pleased if they were shown these documents to say the least. You have my demand and it will be actioned by Friday next.' He walked past Hugh and let himself out.

How dare he refer to me as Hugh, the audacity and the impudence. Hugh was momentarily blinded by his fury at being assaulted by this boy whom he welcomed into his house, who had befriended Teddy and Sophie. He always thought there was something not right with Anthony. How right he had been.

Hugh picked up the telephone to call Larsson.

As Anthony drove back to his mother's he was thinking ahead of what had just taken place, to the flat he would buy in London once the arrangements had been completed. He would use his equity in Madison & Chapman to secure the loan for the flat that would be easily serviced by his salary. Harvey Engineering was their biggest client and he had studied every transaction over the past years. He knew it backwards, warts and all. There was so much unseen potential that he would need to address.

It never occurred to Anthony that Hugh wouldn't meet his demands especially when the original documents were in his safe keeping. Anthony noticed without surprise that the archive box had been removed before had arrived for work on Monday morning.

Julie was pleased to see him as usual although she noticed he seemed more preoccupied than usual. As courteous as ever he never purposely misled Julie but on the other hand he never confided in her. It never crossed his mind. It was not what he said but more what he didn't say that set the basis of their relationship, at least for Julie. Anthony didn't see it as a relationship. They didn't make love that week and now it was Friday.

'Anthony, can you come into the office please.' Harald Larsson led the way ushering Anthony into his office where Hugh sat. Larsson sat at his desk.

'Anthony, Mr Matthews and I have come up with a proposal for you in regards to your position and future here. I am not sure we are doing the right thing but as Mr Matthews explained, we need to move with the times, introducing new young blood into the company. As a result you are to be appointed as assistant managing director to myself with appropriate salary. You will also take control of the Harvey Engineering account. I find this most irregular and worrying as while you have an impressive ability you don't have the experience for such a position. It is all set out in the employment agreement.' Larsson seemed dejected as he handed the document to Anthony.

'You will start as of January the first.'

'Thank you Harald, I'll review the agreement.' Larsson was surprised at being addressed by his first name. Times had changed he thought. Hugh, who after all owned the company, had tied his hands in regard to Anthony.

'Do you mind if I speak privately to Anthony, Harald?' Hugh insisted.

Harald left the room.

'Here is a copy of the share transfer and the certificate for fifty percent of the equity in the company. I have also included an agreement that in return for the equity you will return the original and all copies of the documents.'

'Thank you Hugh, I'll review the agreement and get back to you.' Anthony was very relaxed.

'I would prefer if you would sign it now Anthony.'

'I'll get back to you.' Anthony had no intention to sign any agreement with Hugh, which would implicate him in the whole sordid mess.

Hugh stared at Anthony with loathing and cursed him in his mind.

The impact of the new arrangements caused maximum consternation in the office. Those who had been there forever were shocked that the young new staff member had been appointed to such a senior position which had never existed before. There wasn't sense to any of it and it breached convention. It had unnerved everyone.

'What is all this about' Julie had asked Anthony when they were alone.

'Its about change and advancement, the company has to move with the times Julie.'

'But why you in such a senior position without experience.'

'I'm the obvious choice. I haven't been conditioned by the internal system or politics. That's just the way it is.' Anthony refused to discuss it any further. He couldn't understand what her problem was. It didn't bother him in the least, as he needed to focus on moving forward.

Anthony had already selected the apartment and by the end of February he had the keys to the fully furnished rather large two bedroom premises.

Julie had no idea nor had received any indication that Anthony was going to move into his own apartment. It was on the Monday afternoon after work that he broke the news Julie. Anthony had stayed back at work to finish off some accounts for the morning.

'Hi you, working late.' Anthony had let himself in.

'Just here to collect my clothes and odds and ends, I have a taxi waiting downstairs.'

'Where are you going?' Julie was startled and confused.

'I have my own apartment and will be staying there from now on.'

Julie was stunned. Anthony collected his few belonging and dropped his key to the flat on the kitchen table.

'I'll see you at the office tomorrow.' He left leaving Julie standing in the kitchen.

Her mind in turmoil trying to make sense of what had just happened. Feelings of dejection welled up through her. She felt faint as she sat still unable to fathom Anthony walking out like that. What apartment? How could he afford to buy his own place? The questions flowed without answers. She wept unaware that he would probably never darken her doorway again. He didn't even think about it.

5

Harvey Montague was surprised when he was informed that Anthony Drax would be taking over his account. Firstly because he wasn't aware that he was working for Maddison & Chapman. Secondly, he thought he was young and wouldn't have the experience. After reading the letter from Harald Larsson, Harvey called Hugh Matthews.

'Hugh, how the devil are you?'

'Fine Harvey, working too much of course and not playing golf nearly as much as I should.' Hugh actually enjoyed his work and trappings very much and couldn't envisage not doing what he did. Retirement was furthest from his mind.

'Same here Hugh, it's about time we both retired don't you think.' Harvey was tired as the struggle to keep the business in the black was taking its toll. The market was becoming increasingly competitive and keeping up with modernity was almost impossible. At sixty-one he planned to retire within the next few years. Harvey was already financially comfortable and with the prospect of selling the business he would be flush.

'What's this about Anthony Drax?' Hugh knew why he had called.

'It's a new era Harvey. The old guard has to give way to changing times. Young Drax is exceptional and of the calibre we need to take the business forward. You will be pleasantly surprised by what he will bring to your business. Trust me.'

Harvey had grown to trust Hugh, valuing his word and opinion. Anyway he would be out of it soon so nothing to lose.

'If you say so Hugh, I'll look forward to being pleasantly surprised,' laughed Harvey.

'I'll be down your way next Thursday so a good opportunity to catch up if you are available.'

'I'll book a table for one pm at the club Harvey. Looking forward to it.'

Hugh hadn't mentioned being blackmailed by Anthony, as this would disclose that he had made a monumental blunder with not ensuring the agreement was secreted. Since the signing they hadn't discussed the matter and now Harvey was wrongly secure in believing that Hugh had the only original copy in his personal safe at his home. It was better this way.

For the first few months in his new position at Maddison & Chapman Anthony kept a low profile while going through the business and client list with a fine toothcomb. He also did a comprehensive assessment of the staff against the new plan he had developed to expand the client base and improve the productivity overall. At least twenty percent of the clients were too small and not cost effective so they would go. The emphasis will be on bringing in new large company clients rather than the small to medium ones Larsson seemed obsessed with. To do this he had decided to have a business development position as well as business manager to drive the staff. Nine of the existing staff would be replaced and he would become managing director. Larsson would go. Projected turnover would increase by forty percent and margins by twenty percent within three years. This would be assisted by improving technology and client service. He knew that the basics were there and with quite a few tweaks he would make a substantial improvement.

Anthony would present this strategy as fate accompli at the June board meeting. Larsson would leave with immediate effect taking three months salary and an attractive bonus in appreciation for the years of commitment given. Hugh would be briefed beforehand.

It was on the second Thursday, early afternoon in May that Anthony was walking back to the office from a meeting when he noticed a familiar person sitting at the window seat in a small café. He entered, bought a coffee, and sat down next to the person.

'Hello there.'

The person looked up from reading her magazine, looking very puzzled for a second or two.

'My God, what are you doing here?' Sophie's face radiated delight, as she looked him over with approving eyes. He was smartly dressed and well groomed highlighting his handsome features and attractive physic. My, how he had grown up she mused.

'Just passing when I saw you in the window.' Anthony smiled 'Late lunch?' He had noticed the empty plate and half a cup of coffee.'

'No set time for a lunch break for a busy girl I'm afraid.' Sophie swivelled to directly face Anthony, her knees inches away from his thigh. 'This is a pleasant surprise after all this time. You must tell me all. What have you been doing?'

Anthony was curious. Obviously her father hadn't told her a thing about the developments over the past few years and wondered why. He finished his coffee.

'I have to run,' Anthony lied 'How about we meet tomorrow at Gino's for an Italian and we can catch up then?'

Sophie looked at her watch.

'Oh my god! Look at the time! I have to get back but definitely see you Friday. What time?'

'There's a pub just around the corner so lets meet there after work at six thirty for drinks and I'll book a table at Gino's for eight. Italian alright with you?'

'Fine. Six thirty it is then. I think you'll find the pub is called the Red Lion.' Sophie smiled at Anthony as they walked out of the café.

'I'll look forward to drinks and dinner tomorrow then. So good to see you.' Anthony was pleased.

Sophie reached up on her tiptoes, kissed him on the cheek and was gone. Her perfume lingered as Anthony watched her walk away in a well-cut business suit that accentuated her firm shapely figure. Very nice he thought, turned and walked back to the office.

Later that afternoon Hugh, Harald and Anthony, the three board members, met in Harald's office. Harald listen to Hugh and Anthony discuss the business and its performance since the start of the year with business having increased marginally since Anthony had been in a position of authority which he had to admit was commendable although he felt it had shown him to have been sitting on his hands for the past few years. There was no doubt that new blood injected enthusiasm and vigour into the staff. Goals had been set for each of the staff to achieve with weekly staff meetings at which Anthony would address these goals and demand an explanation from the particular staff member if they hadn't achieved them. There were general strategies the staff discussed and voted on, all very democratic, for a traditional and rather staid business. Harald knew his days were numbered although nothing had been said but his intuition was well developed after so many years. In fact, he wasn't that bothered given that he and his wife had been making plans for his retirement.

Anthony noted that again nothing had been said to him about Sophie and he certainly didn't mention to Hugh that he met her just a few hours before.

He watched from the other side of the street as Sophie entered the Red Lion before he crossed entering behind her. She was standing just inside the entrance. The noise was deafening with the Friday evening workers having already started on their second pint that would probably be the last before they headed home for the weekend. He touched her gently on the shoulder causing her to jump and turn sharply bumping into him. He held her sides to steady her before she stepped back into the crowded room.

'You made me jump Mr Drax.' He could smell the same perfume she had worn the previous day although the suit was different. A woman of means thought Anthony but then again she is a Matthews.

'What would you like to drink?' he asked still with his hands on her sides. He could feel the warmth of her slender body. She didn't seem to mind.

'White wine please.'

'Come with me.' He led her to a small table in the corner where the two previous occupants were donning coats ready to leave.

'Wait here and I'll get the drinks.'

Anthony fought through the crush and waited several minutes to be served. Sophie look at him as he stood at the bar thinking how business like he looked wondering where he worked and what had happened to him over the years. He looked so mature and definite, suspecting he had been through much. Her mind drifted back to the boat shed. Anthony placed the drinks on the table.

'What's a nice girl like you doing in a pub like this?' Anthony said with a slight smile.

'I was shanghaied by an unscrupulous scoundrel if you must know.' Sophie looked serious but her eyes were laughing.

'Well now Miss Matthews tell me all.' Anthony was cautious. What could he glean from Miss Matthews, part of the family that was responsible for the demise of his family, the loss of Westwood House while they, in their affluence, lived oblivious to the results of their deeds. The taste was bitter fuelling his animosity that rose in his throat.

Sophie graduated from Cambridge and had completed her articles with Cunningham Law. She was now a registered solicitor with still much to learn. She lived in a small but comfortable flat in South Kensington, funded from her part of a family trust, something she didn't disclose to Anthony. The trust also gave her a monthly allowance plus a car that added to her salary giving a lifestyle far in excess that the average newly qualified solicitor could expect. Sophie talked about her life with confidence and was surprised how much she confided in Anthony but she trusted him as they had history.

'Why not Matthews, Fortescue & Miller?' Anthony was curious.

'Daddy thought it better for me to gain experience on the outside before coming into the firm.'

Anthony listened with polite concentration while Sophie freely talked about herself and family, mostly about herself. Some people liked to tell their story Anthony mused. Actually most do. Anthony had exploited this human characteristic from the start, which gave him most of his business and personal intelligence often to the detriment of the disclosers. Loose lips sink ships he always reminded himself of the adage making sure he never fell into the trap. Keep your cards close to your chest. Teddy was still studying law at Cambridge as he had had a year off during his studies to travel.

'What about yourself Anthony.' Sophie asked as they walked into Gino's. The restaurant was busy with waiters moving between tables with urgency. Their table had been cleaned and reset with menus waiting for them. They ordered after receiving a bottle of Chianti Tenuta San Vito from Tuscany opened to breath.

'This wine is very good Anthony.' Sophie was impressed.

'Nothing much to tell actually, I'm an accountant in a small company that was very traditional but is slowly emerging into the modern world. Day in day out repetitive work is my life. I live in Kensington.' Anthony was purposely circumspect.

'I am curious about what happened with Westwood House and why you moved so suddenly? I visited mummy and daddy one day and you had gone, all very mysterious. Thought I would never see you again.'

'My father had left my mother and disappeared. Therefore no income so mother was forced to sell and move to a property within her means. She is settled and quite happy at the moment. He hadn't seen his mother for three months so didn't really know how she was. He realised he was not that bothered.

'Oh, Anthony, I'm so sorry. How dreadful for your mother. I do hope she's all right. Are you in contact with your father at all?' Sophie laid her hand on Anthony's arm and was genuinely taken aback, feeling that she should give Anthony a hug of empathy.

'No, I never have been really, even when he was here mostly working and living in London, I rarely saw or spoke to him.' His father and cohorts Hugh and Harvey would receive their comeuppance in due course, of this Anthony was sure, it drove him for the time being, a game he was beginning to enjoy. All in good time he said to himself.

The rest of the meal went well with Sophie taking up the conversation while Anthony listened. They realised that they lived within half a mile of each other, either side of Cromwell Road using the same commute system into London and both wondered why they hadn't come across each other before but that's London.

The train pulled into Gloucester Road tube station and they emerged into a dark cloudy night with a definite May chill in the still air. Sophie shuddered as she took hold of Anthony's arm snuggling in close for a minute or two.

Sophie turned and gave Anthony a hug that he tentatively responded to, a modest ploy. They said their goodnights and we must catch up again comments before turning away from each other.

'Anthony, Anthony!' Anthony had only walked twenty or so paces when he heard his name called. He turned to see Sophie running back towards him.

'Just had a thought.' Sophie caught her breath 'There is a small coffee shop called Bertie's on Cromwell Road that serves excellent coffee and the most delicious croissants. Would you like to meet tomorrow morning for breakfast?'

'Yes, I think so.' Anthony hesitated.

'Something else planned?'

'No, I'll look forward to it actually.' Anthony had been meaning to pay his mother a visit but that could wait.

'OK then, let's say nine thirty?' Sophie was pleased she had asked him.

'Nine thirty then, where is it?'

'Left out of the tube station, right at Cromwell and down about a hundred yards.'

'All right, see you tomorrow. Goodnight Sophie.' Anthony turned and walked away without looking back.

Sophie watched him walk away thinking that he made a striking figure but a man who was quite serious and of few words that gave him a very attractive mysterious quality. Very interesting she thought as she turned and walked towards her flat.

On his appointment to a senior position in Maddison & Chapman with his newfound apartment and lifestyle Anthony consolidated his self-independence and authority.

Julie Banks was devastated when he had left her, suffering emotionally, plunging her into mild depression that gave her a sense of worthlessness making it difficult to function at work and day-to-day, weekends were the worse. Her personality went from bubbly to morose. Her colleagues noticed but failed to discuss it with her. It was exactly four weeks after he had left when there was a knock on her door. She opened it to find Anthony standing there. Her heart missed a beat.

'Hello Anthony, what are you doing here?'

'Just thought I'd call in to catch up. Do you mind if I come in?'

'No.' Julie stood aside while Anthony entered the flat then closed the door.

'Would you like a drink?' Without waiting for a response he went into the kitchen to find the opener and two glasses. Julie sat on the sofa.

While they drank wine they talked about everything and nothing sitting close together. When they finished Anthony stood helping Julie up. In silence he ushered her into the bedroom. They undressed and got into the bed where he urgently subjected her to sex without compassion or consideration yet she responded in kind to his frantic actions. They didn't make love they had sex as a function, a cold hard function for two people, one who loved, the other who didn't. Finally they fell into an exhausted sleep and in the morning when Julie woke he was gone. She loved him so much, this cold callous man who showed her no respect or kindness. She had been used but she loved him, an unrequited love. He visited her each month, to repeat the act for which she hated herself for being involved but needed him, as she was addicted, dependent. One Friday he had to travel to Brighton for an overnight business trip convincing Julie to accompany him. It was the best time she'd had in months. They talked on the train journey down and while Anthony was at his meeting she walked around the shops and sat on the boardwalk seat staring far out to sea with a peace and happiness she hadn't felt in months. That evening they had dinner at the hotel restaurant before going to their room. Anthony even relaxed and seemed to enjoy being away from the office. On return Julie felt buoyant, even hopeful that they would rekindle a normal relationship. She didn't see him until Monday at work but there was no comment, smile or glance from Anthony in recognition that they had had any contact over the past few days. Julie settled back down into her hopeless and hopeful life.

Bertie's was a well-appointed café, comfortable and warm with a few couples dotted around. Sophie was sitting near the magazine shelf, something Anthony would never do, as he hated being annoyed by people coming and going. She already had a coffee.

'Croissant?' Anthony asked as he neared the table.

'Yes please.' Smiled Julie as she looked up from the magazine.

They were both wearing trousers and sneakers, Anthony with a polo neck jumper and Julie a blouse and jumper, her overcoat on the back of her chair. They talked as they ate their croissants and drank coffee.

'Would you like to come for a walk as I thought we could wander up to Hyde Park and then see where the afternoon takes us?'

'I have to go to the office so perhaps some other time.' Anthony looked straight at Sophie.

'Oh well, another day then.' They put on their coats and left the café into the bright morning with the chill still in place holding off the expected summer. It was starting to get busy with the morning traffic and people going about their business.

'At least I can offer to cook you dinner if you are free?' Sophie didn't know why she invited him, finally realising that she had nothing planned and the thought of spending the weekend on her own was a bit depressing. She enjoyed his company though.

'Dinner would be good. What time.'

'Seven?' She gave him the address.

'Can we make it eight?' Anthony needed arrangements to be on his terms.

'Eight it is. Look forward to it Anthony. Take care.' Sophie smiled, touched his arm, turned and walked towards Gloucester Road.

Anthony didn't glean any more useful information from their conversation probably because there was nothing else to glean. He was satisfied that Sophie knew nothing about the relationship between Hugh and himself or that they had a partnership in Maddison & Chapman.

The office was deserted which suited Anthony, as he needed to revisit the changes he would present to Hugh and Harald on June the first. Hugh was in his pocket but he would brief him before hand, not out of courtesy but to ensure he was informed and wouldn't require any explanation. This needed to be short, sharp and final. He and the company needed to move on.

Harvey Montague sat in the walled patio known as the suntrap, having brunch with his wife. He had been reading the paper but his mind had drifted to Anthony. It had been a transition from a cautious and wary attitude with Anthony taking over his account, however, that quickly changed when Anthony talked him through a report he had compiled on the previous five years accounts. Anthony had pointed out while there was nothing amiss there were opportunities where some expenditure could have been capitalised and other classified as research and development. The saving in taxation would be significant. There were some restructuring proposals along with savings that could be made with changing reporting procedures and the benefits of Maddison & Chapman and Harvey Engineering working much closer even though the increase in fees to Maddison & Chapman hadn't been included in the report. This boy was good, Harvey thought. Harvey decided that he needed to make an appointment with Anthony to discuss how they move forward on the proposals. Anthony knew it was only a matter of time before Harvey would call.

Sophie opened the door to find Anthony had changed into smart but casual holding a bottle of wine. No flowers, she thought.

'Hi there, come in.'

He smiled. She led him into the kitchen where she was preparing the simple steak with vegetables for their dinner, perfect with a bottle of red.

'Glasses?' Anthony held up the bottle of wine.

'Over there in the cupboard, corkscrew in the draw below. How was your afternoon?'

'Just tidied up a few loose ends ready for next week and you?'

'Relaxed while reading my book, so easy really.' Sophie launched into a summery of the book while Anthony poured the wine.

Sophie chattered about her life at Cunningham Law where she had been made an assistant on a couple of cases. Mainly hack work but you have to start somewhere. As she gave an overview of the cases Anthony thought about Julie, he would need to pay a visit soon. He enjoyed the hold he had over her without thinking what affect it had on her life. It gave him a sense of control or power over someone's life that she could do little about. He would keep her at Maddison & Chapman to keep an eye on her, as she needed to be available to meet his needs.

Anthony sat on the sofa with Sophie and drank tea. Dinner had been quite ordinary but he hadn't come for dinner and was quite aware what was on Sophie's mind. Another conquest in the game of life wouldn't hurt his ego. If only Hugh could see them now.

Sophie snuggled into Anthony just as she had done in the boatshed. She had failed to capture the same feeling she had with Anthony as the boys and men she had had since were inexperienced, over enthusiastic and generally unfulfilling.

'Do you remember the boatshed Anthony?'

'What boatshed?' Anthony laughed to himself.

'You know. Don't be so damn difficult. Come here.' Sophie reached around his neck drawing him to her. He held her, teasing her with his lips, slowly, softly he played with her as her breathing increased in response.

It has been so long, Sophie thought, realising she had been longing to recapture the moment.

Anthony knew what she was looking for as it had been an awakening for them both. In this instance though, he would exploit the situation as it may come in very handy. Who knows? He realise that he viewed such encounters clinically and that the sense of control and power was far more pleasurable than any emotional attachment could possible be.

He repeatedly raised her to near climax before taking her gently down to the most erotic fulfilment she had ever encountered or could ever have dreamed of. He surrendered to her in the early hours of the morning with a strong rhythmic passion that didn't falter as they merged as one within the cocoon of warmth, closeness and erotic pleasure. They were wrapped in each other's arm as they lay sleeping contented and released. In the late morning, Sophie stirred, stretching, when a warm wave of pleasure ran over her at the memory. She looked for Anthony but he was not there.

❖

Hugh, Harald and Anthony sat in silence in Harald's office for the scheduled board meeting, as it was the first of June. A bright sunlit day that smelt of a real summer after a rather dismal spring of frequent rain, cold wind peppered by colder days of cloudy sunshine. Spirits were up, smiles emerging, it was going to be a good day.

Anthony broke the silence.

'Well Harald?'

Ignoring Anthony Harald turned to Hugh.

'Were you involved in the planning of this Hugh?'

Hugh looked directly at Harald.

'No, it is something that Anthony has designed and is going to carry out Harald. Its best for the future of the company and its best for the staff in the long term.' Hugh didn't believe a word of what he had just said. It was only going to be best for Anthony and himself if he was lucky.

'What about the staff you are going to dismiss? For God's sake Hugh they have been here forever and some of them are coming up for retirement surely you just can't put them on the scrap heap? Isn't there a semblance of decency left?'

Harald felt himself sinking. He was tired. There wasn't enough energy left to fight. He sat upright.

'Alright then, if that's they way you want it, I tender my resignation with immediate effect.' Harald didn't believe he had just said that.

'Don't be so hasty Harald, give it some thought. Sleep on it. I am sure you'll feel differently in the morning.' Hugh wasn't expecting Harald's resignation.

Anthony shuffled through the papers in front of him withdrawing two sheets placing one in front of Harald and a copy in front of Hugh. It was Harald's resignation. All he needed to do was to sign it.

'You're a callous little bastard' Harald spat. Hugh was stunned.

'Now listen here,' Hugh said to Anthony who sat relaxed and expressionless. Anthony said nothing.

'Leave it Hugh.' Harald signed the resignation letter. Strangely, he felt some relief. 'I want to convert my options and want a healthy goodwill payment for the years of service.' Harald knew he was beaten. He wanted out.

'Lets have an early lunch Harald and we'll discuss your exit.' They rose. Harald put his overcoat on and picked up his brief case. Anthony stood.

'Your office keys please Harald. I'll have your personal effects sent to you. You will not come back to the office under any circumstance.' Anthony held out his hand.

Harald looked at Anthony's hand for a moment before he reached into his pocket, removed the keys throwing them on his desk, Anthony's desk. Turned and walked out of the office without another word. Hugh followed.

Anthony spent the next hour or two cleaning out Harold's bits and pieces arranging them to be couriered to his home address. He sat at the desk looking around the office. It will need to be completely refurbished. Out with the old in with the new. Looking through Harald's share option agreement he suddenly smiled to himself. The options were only valid if exercised before resignation. The options reverted to the company's option trust that now held twenty percent of total shares. It was a no brainer. Anthony would allot the twenty percent to himself immediately. As his fifty percent of gifted shares from Hugh were non-dilutable he would hold seventy percent of the company giving him control. Hugh could do nothing about it; actually, he wouldn't even need Hugh or a board of directors. An enviable position, life was getting better by the moment. He started the procedure immediately.

By the time Hugh got back to Anthony with the proposal for Harald's share options and goodwill payment, the company was already under Anthony's control. Anthony processed Harald's good will payment not for Harald but as a bonus payment for himself that paid off fifty percent of his mortgage. He also amalgamated his and Harald's salaries to give what he saw as a justifiable salary level befitting his managing director position. Harald walked away with nothing.

When Hugh learnt what Anthony had engineered he was furious, turning to despair with realisation that there was nothing he could do about it. Hugh's worst suspicions about Anthony had been confirmed. Finally he realised that Anthony would go to any length to feather his own nest at the expense of anyone and everyone. He was truly an evil, conniving scoundrel, Hugh didn't swear, he just felt ill.

By the end of July, planned staff dismissals and new appointments had been made. Twenty percent of clients had been given notice with new client recruitment well underway. The company hadn't suffered any drop in revenue but actually gained five percent. All was going according to plan. Julie had been retained being of very good use several times in relatively quick succession. She hated herself.

Hugh never mentioned Sophie nor did he indicate that he new anything about her relationship with Anthony. Anthony suspected Sophie hadn't told her parents and as such was comfortable with a clandestine relationship. They both worked long hours and contact during the week was minimal so it was kept to Saturday evening with the infrequent restaurant meal, mostly it was Sophie preparing a meal at her flat. Anthony would stay the night and they would breakfast at Bertie's on Sunday morning. In a relatively short time the settled routine suited them and their busy lives. Anthony, without explanation, ensured he broke the routine from time to time. He was never questioned.

'Mr Drax, I have a Mr Montague on line one.'

'Harvey, how are you?'

'Fair to middling Anthony, when are you coming to Peterborough next?'

'Hang on and I'll check.' Anthony opened his diary.

'Wednesday next week actually, anything the matter?'

'No, not at all, to the contrary, the business has improved since you have taken the reins of our account.' Harvey paused. 'I was thinking that there might be some way to work closer than we are currently. Can you give it some thought and we'll discuss it next Wednesday.'

'Sure thing Harvey, look forward to catching up. I have the end of last month's accounts as well. Not bad.' Anthony had already thought about it, many times.

'Okay then. Take care. By the way are you staying over?'

'No, its up and back visit, see you then.'

'Okay.' Harvey hung up.

Anthony walked into the office to where Julie was sitting.

'Miss Banks could you come into my office please?'

Julie looking startled followed him into his office and stood at his desk.

'Sit down Julie.' She sat down on the edge of one of the two new chairs facing his desk. The office had been stripped of the clutter since Harald had gone, with the wood panels receiving a clean and polish. New carpet, desk and chairs, otherwise just as it was but minimalist as was the cost.

'Miss Banks, I will be going to Peterborough next Wednesday and would like you to accompany me as my assistant.'

Julie's heart skipped a beat. She so longed for these infrequent trips, which she was forever hopeful, would rekindle the wonderful relationship they first had.

'Yes Mr Drax, I'll tell the business manager that I will be accompanying you. Thank you.' She had suddenly brightened up with a slight smile on her lips.

'No. You will request a day off for personal reasons on Monday. No one is to know you will be coming with me. I'll meet you at Kings Cross at eight sharp. Train leaves at eight fifteen. Thank you Miss Banks, close the door behind you.'

'Yes Mr Drax.' Julie closed the door behind her. How could he be so cruel Julie thought? Should I refuse to go and tell him its over? She knew she would go, as she couldn't help herself.

'Hello Anthony, how are you?' Anthony entered Harvey's office. The trip to Peterborough was uneventful. Anthony and Julie talked little on the way up and he told her to spend time in town and he would meet her at the Great Northern Hotel at two pm.

'Very well thank you Harvey.'

They discussed lasts months accounts and business performance since the start of the year. Then spent time going over the proposals Anthony had submitted previously. Much of it was common sense and would take little to implement.

 'Have you given any thought to how we move ahead with all this and more in the future Anthony.'

'Its simple, you will appoint me as finance director and of course I'll have a board position. You will pay me thirty thousand pounds per annum plus expenses and one thousand pounds per month directors fee. I will be gifted ten percent of the company equity with another sixteen percent unrestricted options. I will receive an annual bonus of five percent of annual growth. All will be paid into my private account.'

'But I already have a finance director.' He's not only good but outrageously audacious thought Harvey.

'He will need to go and I will appoint a financial controller.'

'Look Anthony, I'll need to give it some thought and let you know.' Harvey wasn't going to be rushed.

'I will be leaving in fifteen minutes, that's enough time don't you think?'

Harvey rose and shook Anthony's hand.

'It's a deal then Anthony. Now go before you come up with anything else.' Laughed Harvey.

Anthony walked through the entrance of the Great Northern Hotel at precisely two pm to see Julie sitting in the foyer. He walked to the receptionist collected his key and went to the elevator. Julie followed.

Maddison & Chapman went from strength to strength engaging new lucrative clients while dispensing the older low margin clients. No room for loyalty to clients' only maximising profits from increasing turnover. For Anthony it was about how much he could draw from the business, which was growing at an admirable rate. His private account was growing with regular payments from Harvey engineering that were reinvested into blue chip high return stock. All was going according to plan.

After the initial reservations Harvey had about the unorthodox demands of Anthony, he was coming around to the realisation that it had been a good move. There had been positive changes throughout the organisation in communication, quoting for projects, accounting and hiring and firing. All was brought into the central office at Peterborough that gave a substantial reduction in the spread of senior and middle management saving the company thousands of pounds while increasing productivity and profits. Anthony would receive a hefty bonus for his first year but not quite as much as Harvey would pay himself. Yes, Harvey was happy.

Hugh berated himself daily in having made such a fundamental blunder allowing someone like Anthony to find such incriminating documents. He hadn't told Harvey or Henry but knew they would find out sooner than later which would cause more grief than he could imagine for his negligence. Damn Anthony and damn himself was his daily mantra that ate through every fibre in his body and clouded his mind. The usually confident clear thinking rational solicitor, senior partner of Matthews, Fortescue & Miller was inundated with extreme thoughts of reclamation that only a desperate man could have. Anthony had stolen Maddison & Chapman from him, Hugh believed, completely missing the irony and now he was a constant threat, a thorn in the side that must be extracted and discarded. He had to, somehow, heal the wound before it got totally out of hand. How dare Anthony remove him as a director and water down his share holding. Anthony owned seventy percent of the company putting him in absolute control. The biggest threat was to his position in the legal practice, his standing in the community and to his family. The thought of it consumed him.

Over the months the guilt and anger Hugh held was slowly projected onto Anthony. He demonised the young Anthony. It was his entire fault without question. He must do something before Anthony struck again.

6

The year was coming to a close as they moved into December having been through a mild autumn with its magnificent display of red brown and yellow leaves cascading throughout the country. The winter chill had crept in with commuters well rugged up against the impending onset of colder times.

Sophie had not seen or heard from Anthony for two weeks but wasn't unduly worried. There was a knock on her door.

'Hello stranger.' Sophie said without conviction as Anthony entered her flat with a bottle of red wine, chocolates and flowers. This is first, mused Sophie.

'What's the celebration for?'

'Have been caught up with work so thought a reunion would be in order.' Anthony said candidly. Sophie laughed.

'Just as well my friend, you're one lucky boy.' Anthony hated being called boy and would only tolerate it from Sophie, at least for the time being.

Anthony never asked Sophie either about work, socially or herself personally. Not that there was much to tell with the crazy hours she kept at Cunningham Legal and as far as social life went there was only the infrequent cup of coffee with a girl friend or two to catch up on the latest gossip and the odd visit to see her parents without mention of Anthony from either side of course. She wasn't quite sure why that was. Given that her father worked in London she thought she would see more of him but it never seemed to happen though they talked on the phone from time to time.

Her mother and father loved her and Teddy dearly as they were kind, caring and considerate children. Always had been.

They chattered over dinner and afterwards sat on the sofa with coffee while Sophie nibbled a chocolate. Anthony didn't eat chocolates.

'By the way I have an early Christmas present for you.' Sophie looked at Anthony with a slight smile on her lips.

'I'm always up for a Christmas present.' Anthony relaxed and closed his eyes.

'I'm pregnant.'

Anthony didn't react, sitting with eyes closed as if he hadn't heard. This could be interesting he thought.

'Have you told your parents?'

'Not yet.'

'Well that's a turn up for the books.' Anthony sat up and smiled at Sophie. 'Congratulations Sophie Matthews.' He held her head with both hands kissed her lightly.

'Congratulations to both of us wouldn't you say Mr?'

'Definitely Mrs'

Sophie snuggled into him.

'Are you going to make an honest woman out of me?'

'Well now that's a thought.' Anthony said with underlying lightness.

'Well are you?'

'Would you like that?'

'Its only the decent thing to do now that you have taken advantage of me and got me in the family way.'

'So you had nothing to do with it then?' Laughed Anthony.

'Not in the slightest, it was all your doing you scoundrel. You should be tarred and feathered before being run out of

town for such a dastardly deed. You're such a horrible person you know.'
'I know, my entire fault. What to do is the question. Either I do a runner or get burdened with a ball and chain. Decisions, decisions, decisions.' Anthony had already made up his mind. This was going to be a massive blow to Hugh. Anthony was delighted. Of course he would marry Sophie.
'How far pregnant are you?' Anthony sat up and looked seriously at Sophie.
Sophie's heart sank.
'Just under three months.'
'Come to bed and I'll give you my decision.'
They held each other under the warm covers with Sophie's head nesting in the crook of Anthony's neck. She kissed his neck softly.
'Well what's the verdict?'
'Yes, I will marry you.' Anthony said simply.
Sophie hadn't expected it would turn out as easy as this. She wasn't sure she wanted to get married but now that he had said yes she would go through with it. Here goes my career, at least for the foreseeable future, she thought. God, do I really want to be a mother? A feeling of dread shivered through her.
They went to Bertie's for breakfast, the usual coffee and croissants. There was a new feeling in the air. Their relationship had changed. They both knew it.
'When are you going to tell your parents?' Anthony had waited to put the question.
'I am spending a few days over Christmas with them and thought I would tell them then. Would you like to join us for Christmas?'

'I would love to but I am spending it with my mother. She hasn't anyone else to support her.'

'Of course, sorry, I should have realised.' Sophie hadn't met Anthony's mother since they had left Westwood but didn't doubt she would very soon, probably in the New Year.

'Any thoughts on wedding dates?' He wasn't really bothered as long as it didn't interfere with his business.

'Early January before I look like a balloon. Just a small family wedding at St Mary's Church in Teddington with the reception at The Alexander Hotel, a private room, what do you think?'

'I'll leave it to you. Out of my comfort zone I'm afraid. It'll be fine whatever you decide Sophie.' Anthony couldn't care less where, what or how, just as long as Hugh was there, the old stuffy fop who he had firmly in place and under control. He didn't trust him though and now he would be further locked in, as he wouldn't, couldn't do anything but welcome Anthony with open arms into the family without his dastardly deeds coming to light. No Hugh, I've got you for as long as I want you. Anthony couldn't believe his luck. As far as Sophie goes, she was intelligent, interesting and good fun. Most of all she was useful as she gave him security and strength in the scheme of things, especially for what he had in mind. He felt invincible as they got up from the table and put on their coats, it was cold outside.

'Coming back with me?' Sophie asked hopefully.

'Afraid not, work tomorrow and much to prepare for.' He gave her a hug and kissed her longingly. 'See you during the week.' Anthony turned and walked away without looking back. Nothing changed Sophie thought.

It was nine in the evening when he knocked on Julie's door. The door opened to a gaunt and morose woman who didn't resemble the Julie he had first met. Without expression she turned and walked into the bedroom.

London, with its overcast sky and cold winds, buzzed with a throng of Christmas shoppers crowding into brightly lit shops draped with Christmas lights and decorations. People were running to and fro, businesses frantically competing for the end of year sales. It will soon be another year that will throw up new challenges and experiences that for Anthony gave him the adrenalin rush he so yearned for. He knew it would be a memorable year not only because he was to marry Sophie with a baby on the way, somewhat incidental to his plans, but also there were bigger fish to fry. It was all about timing. This time he would more than double his assets and personal revenue while adding a few more enemies to the growing list that he ignored, consequence of war he would say to himself.

Anthony parked outside his mothers flat in his new Bentley S3 Continental. He took out her presents and the hamper that held a bottle of champagne. They chattered for an hour or so before he told her that he and Sophie were to be married in January at St Mary's Church. She was surprised but nonplussed, as she didn't even know that he had anything to do with the Matthews family these days. He didn't go into detail. His mother had withdrawn over the past few years and was losing reality fast, maybe some sort of dementia he thought. How long she would last was anyone's guess. He couldn't bring himself to spend Christmas or any other time with her, as conversation was inane with fluctuating moods but mostly silence. Anthony was comfortable with his own company. After goodbyes he drove back to the London garage he had rented, near his apartment. Must be the most expensive piece of real estate in the area given the extortionate cost. He would buy it or something similar as soon as possible. An exploiter can't tolerate being exploited.

He caught the tube into the city after having decided he would spend Christmas Eve with the few friends he had made there. Permanent fixtures, he called them, only in small doses, just bearable after a few drinks. They weren't friends; they were clients, as Anthony didn't have any friends, not even Sophie. He would enjoy spending Christmas day on his own isolated from the nonsense of the world. He would read, listen to music and have a bottle or two of his best red wine. Anthony had received an invitation from Harvey Montague to come for lunch on Boxing Day, so taking his new Bentley would give it a good run as well as impressing Harvey.

Sophie was comfortable at Teddington Manor surrounded by fond memories of childhood. Nothing had changed, that was the beauty of it. Even her family hadn't really changed she observed as they sat in the sitting room that looked over the lawn stretching down to the boat shed perched on the edge of the Thames with its shimmering dirty brown water under the grey sky.

Mother, father and Teddy were chatting quietly, drinks in hand, as she looked on with a warm feeling of love for these wonderful people in her life. Since graduating she had not contacted them nearly enough, which hadn't made any difference really.

"Listen up! I have something very important to tell you before we get into our Christmas celebrations proper.' The bright joyous Christmas tree blinked its colourful lights with excitement while safeguarding the presents underneath its foliage. The chatter stopped with all looking at her attentively. They did love her.

'Well my girl, what important news do you bring?' Chortled Hugh.

'You know since I went to work with Cunningham Legal I haven't had time to breath or spend time with my family. So it's lovely to be with you for the next few days especially at Teddington Hall.'

'Is that it?' Exclaimed Teddy.

'Not quite Teddy, now do be quiet and give me a chance, please.'

They refocused feigning much seriousness.

'It hasn't been all work and no play though. I have been seeing someone for a considerable time. It has become very serious recently so thought I had better let the family in on the matter.'

They family sat looking stunned with jaws dropped, making the whole scene quite comical. Sophie laughed.

'Come on, it's a relationship not the plague.'

Jumbled questions were fired thick and fast.

'Hold on.' Sophie held up her hand. 'Before we get into the small print there is a complicating factor. I am pregnant and before I start to look like a barrel we are going to get married at St Mary's Church on January the twenty fourth.

You are all invited of course.' There was no other way to say it.

At least that stopped the questions thought Sophie.

Hugh spoke first.

'And who is the man lucky enough to have captured your heart?'

'Anthony Drax.'

The silence was deafening, the reactions confusing. Her mother slumped and looked at the floor, her father paled and looked positively ill, only Teddy spoke.

'You're pregnant to Anthony Drax! For Christ's sake Sophie he's my age. What is he doing these days? Where did you meet him?'

The eighteen thirty-two pulled into Brighton station. Raymond and Clare Banks waiting on platform two didn't recognise their daughter as she disembarked. It was only when she approached they realised that this very thin, old looking, unsmiling woman was their daughter.

'Oh Julie what's happened to you? You've lost so much weight.' Clare failed to find the words. Her mother's concern was heart breaking. Julie could say nothing.

Raymond Banks picked up his daughter's case.

'Come on, let's go home.'

7

It was a cold, damp overcast day as the Bentley sped up the A1 towards Peterborough. Anthony had spent Christmas day going through his New Year strategy for Harvey Engineering but that could wait. Timing was everything. The Bentley was an important symbol of success for Anthony, albeit at the expense of others but business is business. He left the A1 for the A605 towards Warmington. The rather grand entrance with its ancient stone pillars loomed on the left. He wound his way up the tree-lined driveway that finally broke through onto a manicured field that surrounded the large grey granite building with slate roof. It looked well kept, homely and warm with widows well lit on this dull day. There were several other cars on the driveway at the front of the house as Anthony came to a stop.

Harvey was standing in front of the warm open fire talking to two of his guests as he noticed through the large front clear leaded window the Bentley coming towards the house. A smart but casually dressed Anthony got out of the car carrying a bottle of wine and flowers walked to the front door. The doorbell chimed.

He has certainly come along way in a very short time, young and confident but he is very good at what he does thought Harvey. Harvey opened the door.

'Anthony, come in out of the cold. Good to see you and thanks for coming.'

'Thanks for having me Harvey. I've been looking forward to coming up.'

Harvey took Anthony's cashmere overcoat as he ushered him into the main front reception room. Introductions were made, drinks refreshed, as they settled back into conversations.

'No Mrs Drax?'

Anthony turned to the beautiful young woman who had come up to him from the side.

'Not yet I'm afraid and you are?'

'Beth Russell.' She held out her hand that he took firmly, feeling the soft warmth. Not bad he thought.

'Call me Anthony. So where do you fit in.'

'I am the youngest sibling of the Montague clan. My husband is spending Christmas in New York, lucky fellow.'

All the better for me Anthony thought. They chattered until the call for lunch was made.

'As we don't have partners mother has sat us together.'

Beth showed Anthony to their places at the table. The sumptuous luncheon was very pleasant as was the company. Anthony purposely stopped at one glass of wine and then settled on water with a slice of lemon. Beth was impressed, as her husband would have been quite inebriated by now which would have triggered the raucous behaviour she loathed. One of the characteristics he was well known and mocked for, she hated him for it.

As the luncheon party withdrew to the sitting room for coffee and tea Anthony made his apologies; he needed to get back to London. He had only briefly talked to Harvey, no mention of work though. Beth walked him to the door.

'I come to London from time to time and was wondering if you would be available for a tea one afternoon.'
'It would be a pleasure Beth.'
Anthony gave Beth his business card. They said goodbye and she watched him as he drove away. It could have been so different thought Beth. She smiled to herself.

'So your Christmas was quiet then? How is your mother?'
Sophie had called Anthony at work inviting him around for dinner on Wednesday.
'Yes. She's fine, nothing new there. Yours was interesting then.'
'As I said when I called you, the reaction to our pending marriage was startling to say the least. You would think I was some sixteen-year-old idiot who had never made a decision before in her life. It was weird Anthony, completely out of character for my family. I thought father was going to have a seizure. The whole Christmas was a disaster. As for the pregnancy, well.'
Probably more like a heart attack, Anthony smiled.
'At least mother is helping me with the wedding arrangements. You had better press your tux.'
'Already done.' Anthony took her in his arms and kissed her long and passionately. They had dinner later that evening after having made urgent love, which Anthony knew, would dissolve any concerns or doubts Sophie may have developed over Christmas.
Julie never did return to work.
The wedding went off remarkably well given Hugh was incandescent at the thought of Sophie marrying Anthony. Only the Matthews and his mother were present at the

church and reception, which was a quiet affair without speeches so all was done and dusted by ten o'clock in the evening. They drove back to Sophie's flat where Anthony spent the rest of the week. They had decided that they would keep the same arrangements while they sorted out a home into which they would move when Sophie had the baby. Anthony would arrange everything beforehand.

Sophie had also signed the prenuptial agreement without too much discussion, although she thought it was a little unusual. She never mentioned it to her parents.

Anthony kept the businesses on an even keel to ensure that growth rates were maintained and showed healthy profits. The only change was that Maddison & Chapman took the whole of the floor above them when it became available for rent. Minimal refurbishment with only four staff moving in as it was to accommodate planned expansion, commensurate with the good work practises. His business development manager was proving his worth. Bit of a wiz this chap. Anyone who made money for Anthony was a bit of a wiz. Anthony's one big coup d'état was to convince Harvey to transfer all administrative and financial functions to Maddison & Chapman. While it saved a substantial amount for Harvey Engineering, it increased revenue a massive ten percent for his company. He knew Harvey had underestimated the control he had sacrificed. There was more to come.

Emma Drax was born on the twenty first of July. An uncomplicated, uneventful seven pounds ten ounces birth, mother and baby were both well.

Anthony Drax stood looking out of the hospital window with unseeing eyes. Immersed in his thoughts. He was not really that interested in the birth. His preoccupation was work.

'Anthony!'

Anthony was jolted out of his thoughts and slowly turned to face Sophie in the hospital bed. A comfortable private room in Teddington Memorial Hospital only the best.

'Sorry Sophie, miles away' responded Anthony 'what did you say'

'Are you pleased with Emma?'

Anthony looked at the bundle Sophie was holding. A daughter.

'Of course I am Sophie. She's delightful.'

'You said you have a house for us to move into when I get out of hospital, is that so?'

'Ah, the surprise, yes it's true and rest assured you will be surprised and more than pleased.'

'This is very unusual you know. Not knowing where Emma and I are to end up. It could be on the street for all I know.' Sophie smiled.

'Slightly better than being on the streets, but only just.' Anthony teased.

'What about all my goods and chattels, my friend.'

'Your flat has been completely cleared out with all goods and chattels safely installed in the new premises. Except for everything that you requested to be disposed of.'

'What do you mean disposed of?'

'Just kidding' laughed Anthony 'no, everything safe and sound.

'Well, I wish you would tell me.' Sophie scowled. Anthony seemed unusually bright and cheerful, definitely less serious.

'All in good time, you are in here for another four days.'
Mrs Matthews and Hugh walked into the room.
'Mrs Matthews, Hugh.' He nodded politely.
'Hello Anthony.' Mrs Matthews walked over and gave him a kiss on the cheek.
Hugh ignored him.
'Mummy, Daddy, so lovely to see you.'
'Hello darling.' Mrs Matthews and Hugh kissed and hugged their special only daughter.
Hugh took Emma from Sophie and gazed lovingly at her.
'Well, I'm on my way, so I'll say goodnight Sophie.' Anthony walked over and kissed her.
'Goodnight darling, see you soon?'
'Of course, I'll call you tomorrow.'
'Goodbye Mrs Matthews, Hugh.'
'Goodbye Anthony.' Mrs Matthews gave him another kiss on the cheek as she prudently hugged him. She did try to be civil to him after all he is her son in law.
Hugh continued to ignore him.
'Mr Drax, I have Elizabeth Russell on the line for you.'
'Who?' Anthony didn't know Elizabeth Russell.
'Elizabeth Russell, she said it was a personal call.'
'Thank you put her through.'
'Hello, Anthony Drax.'
'Hi Anthony, it's Beth Russell. How are you?'
'Fine Beth, I'd given up waiting for your call.' He had gone blank for a minute.
'I know, sorry about that. Since Christmas I've been to London twice and both times with David so a bit difficult I'm afraid.'
'You're on your own this time?'

'Yes, David has gone to New York for two weeks and as I am here I thought we could catch up. How are you for time?'

'Where are you staying?'

'The Lanes Park, it's not our usual but thought it would make a pleasant change. A girl needs to treat herself now and again' Anthony was impressed.

'I know it well. Would you be available for dinner this evening, the Lanes Park has an excellent restaurant, I'll book us in for eight.'

Straight to the point thought Beth.

'Lovely. I'll meet you in the foyer. Let's have a drink in the bar say seven thirty. Looking forward to it Anthony.'

'Me too Beth, bye.'

Anthony called Sophie at the hospital to tell her he had a business engagement at the club this evening if she wanted him. She would never call the club. They chatted about Emma. Sophie wanted to know where the new house was but Anthony wouldn't disclose.

True to her word Beth was waiting in the foyer when he arrived at seven thirty, more beautiful than he remembered. She stood a slim proud five six, with long blond straight hair and a sheer black evening dress complimented by a thin silver chain necklace. Her skin was clear with striking facial features brought to light by that sensual smile and all alone, you silly boy David, Anthony thought as he walked confidently up to her. The perfume fragrance that met Anthony was seductive.

Beth had seen Anthony come into the foyer before he had seen her. A striking figure of a man in a well cut dark grey dinner suit, white shirt and designer tie. His good-looking features took her breath away. Nothing like David, thank God. They had both made the effort to dress for the occasion. She suspected he always did.

'Beth, so good to see you.' He held her shoulders lightly and kissed each cheek.

'You too Anthony.' Immediately enjoying his closeness. 'A drink at the bar.'

'Of course.'

Beth tucked her hand into his arm as they walked through the palatial lush foyer towards the softly lit moody bar where several couples sat in secluded booths deep in quiet conversation. Several women looked at this rather beautiful couple for seconds before turning their envious eyes back.

'Let's sit at the bar Anthony.' Beth smiled.

The bar stools were functional and comfortable. Good choice thought Anthony. The barman took the order for a gin and tonic and a vodka martini. Beth took a sip of her gin and tonic then looked at Anthony giving him another very sensual smile. Anthony hadn't touched his drink nor had his gaze left Beth.

'This is very cosy Mr Drax.' Beth looked ravishing and knew it.

Anthony had a niggling suspicion that there was more to this, although not quite sure. He would wait to see how she played her cards.

'Very cosy indeed.' Anthony picked up his martini.

'Have you known Harvey very long?'

'Not that long, my company handles some of his accounting functions.'

Beth knew more than she let on so it was going to be a cat and mouse game. Anthony smiled.

'My husband also does some work for Harvey, something to do with export. He has more than one client of course but he does value the work he does with Harvey. Do you know David?'

David Russell was one of three agents handling exports for Harvey Engineering but he was the least successful in that he had the most problems, which had caused Harvey Engineering some angst over the past few years. Anthony had him marked for the chopping block due to his incompetence and belligerent attitude when he over indulged, which was often. Not good for the company.

'I have met your husband before. Although I don't have anything to do with the export side of the business.'

Wait for it.

'I thought you might have met him. David has been struggling lately as he lost a couple of accounts and can't seem to replace them. He's hoping to get more of the Harvey Engineering business, what do you think?'

Before Anthony could respond a waiter carrying a silver try came up to them.

'Mr Drax, your table is ready. Would you follow me please.'

The waiter collected their unfinished drinks while Anthony and Beth stood then followed the waiter. Beth placed her hand on Anthony's arm again.

The dinner was relaxed and pleasant with the nouvelle cuisine as good as ever. Anthony held back on the wine leaving Beth to consume most of the bottle. He steered them away from talk about work and David that seemed to be acceptable for Beth. Let her talk thought Anthony as he sat back listening to her chatter.

'Would you like to come up to my room for a nightcap Anthony?'

'I think one of those booths near the bar would be a great way to finish off the evening. Afterwards I'll walk you to your door.'

Beth seemed to be enjoying herself as she continued to talk her way to the booth snuggling unashamedly into Anthony as they sat down. The waiter appeared.

'Can I take your order Mr Drax?'

'What would you like Beth?'

'I'll have champagne.' Beth had probably had enough.

'Champagne and a TG&T for me.' The waiter left for the bar.

Anthony's TG&T is a gin and tonic without the gin always ordered when he wanted to keep a clear head. An understanding he had established at Lanes Park. Beth had missed the order as most did.

Beth leaned heavily on Anthony as he walked her to her hotel room.

'You know you are more than welcome to come in Anthony.'

Not tonight Josephine Anthony thought.

'Thank you Beth but I have to go away tomorrow so need to get back and pack, early start.' Beth showed her disappointment.

Anthony roughly grabbed both her shoulders, pulled her up and slowly but gently kissed her deeply for a full minute. Beth crumpled into his arms returning his advances with equal measure. She was ready for everything.

'Please.' Beth whispered against his chest as her arms snaked around him to hold him firmly against her. Anthony was aroused but determined.

He pulled her away, holding her at arms length. Contact was important.

'Will you still be here Monday?'

'Yes.' Beth said hesitantly.

'Order a light evening snack with a bottle of champagne for nine thirty. I'll be here at seven thirty.' Beth seemed confused.

'All right Anthony, can't you come Saturday or even tomorrow?'

'I'll be back on Monday. Goodnight Beth.'

He kissed her softly but passionately before leaving her standing at the door. As the lift door closed he glimpsed Beth entering her room giving an expressionless sideglance as she went. If you're a good girl we'll see what happens Monday, Anthony thought. David gets nothing but maybe I get Beth.

❖

Sophie sat in the front passenger's seat of the Bentley holding Emma as Anthony closed her door gently. As they drove away from the hospital Sophie seemed unusually quiet. It was a beautiful clear sunny day without being unduly hot. The sky was bluer, the grass greener and generally all was good with the world.

'I'm so pleased to be out of there even though it was a well earned rest after giving birth to this special little girl. I'm so happy Anthony; she's such a darling, so very special. Don't you think?'

'Of course I do Sophie.' He never called her darling or love or any other endearment. It didn't really bother her though.

'Well baby girl we're going home wherever home is.' She looked at Anthony. 'Well, where is home?'

'Be patient. You'll see soon enough.'

Sophie looked at Emma and chattered as they drove east towards the Thames. It was only when they turned north into Manor Road that she sensed something and looked up.

'Oh my God, were are we going?'

When they entered Twickenham Road she became increasingly concerned. Emma stirred.

'Anthony, don't you dare tell me we are going to live with mother and father.'

'Close.' Anthony teased

Anthony slowed and turned right into the driveway. Sophie froze.

'What is this about Anthony?'

The Bentley slowly pulled up in front of Westwood House.

'Welcome home.' Anthony was beaming. Sophie was stunned.

'What are we doing here Anthony.' Sophie was stoned faced looking directly at Anthony. Emma was asleep.

'Sophie, this is our new home. Come inside and I'll explain.' Anthony opened the car door, walked around to Sophie and opened her door.

'Come on you'll be more surprised when you get inside.'

Sophie stood in the entrance hall of Westwood House, holding Emma as she gazed about. The traditional features of the house had been kept and fully restored along with everything else having been tastily modernised to give the feel of a new build that had captured traditional elements or was it the other way around, Sophie wasn't sure but whatever it was it totally defused her. It was amazing.

'This is unbelievable. Whose house is it Anthony? Are you renting it?'

'No, I bought it and had it totally refurbished ready for us to move into.'

'But how, when?'

Anthony explained that when he was looking for a suitable home Westwood House came up for sale. The people who bought it from his mother had it heavily mortgaged against their business that ran into difficulties. They were forced by the bank to sell it quickly so Anthony was able to buy it for seventy five percent of what his mother had sold it for.

What he didn't tell Sophie was that he had to use his apartment and Maddison & Chapman as collateral for a hefty mortgage. His mother agreed to sell her flat to provide the deposit conditional to her moving in using the annex his grandmother had lived in. Anthony estimated he would repay his mortgage within three years when he would own it outright. He had cash savings that allowed him to fund the restoration and modernisation that gave him an asset worth double of what he paid, a very good investment, neatly wrapped in his name only.

'I want to show you the upper rooms first.' Anthony ushered her up the grand staircase. Again, Sophie was overwhelmed by the quality of the work and the décor that was perfect to her taste.

'How did you get everything so perfect?'

'You forget I have spent many a hour in your flat, also listening to your thoughts and ideas of the perfect home.'
'Wow, you certainly got it right Anthony. It's just beautiful. So functional and liveable, I don't know what to say.'
'Don't say anything.'
They went back down to the kitchen that was new throughout and completely took Sophie's breath away. It was when they went into the second reception room that Sophie received her greatest surprise. A well-dressed elderly woman sat in the sunny bay window reading a book, oblivious to all until she realised they had entered. She turned and rose out of the lounge chair.
'Mrs Drax, how nice to meet you.' Sophie hadn't been expecting to see her.
'Hello dear, lovely to see you and this must be Emma.' She looked curiously at the bundle in Anthony's arms.
'Hello mother, everything alright?'
'Yes dear, I've settled in well and feel very comfortable. It's so nice to be home again.' Rosemary smiled. 'And to have you all living here with me will be just perfect.'
Sophie looked at Anthony.
'Mother is an investor in Westwood House and will be living in the annex where grandmother lived. You'll have company while I'm in London or travelling on business.'
Sophie had much to take in.
Just as she was about to respond Anthony cut in.
'I have also employed two full time housekeepers come cooks and a part time gardener to keep all in order. Until you get settled, I've hired an au pair to assist you with Emma. They all start Monday. Everything has been taken care of although we can iron out any difficulties as we

progress.' Always the businessman Sophie laughed to herself but he is very thoughtful and considerate; I didn't expect this, at all.

'Thank you darling, you have taken care of everything perfectly. I'll have Mrs Drax to keep me company and mummy is just up the road. Just perfect.' She smiled warmly at Rosemary not sure how this was going to turn out.

'I just need to go to the den for an hour. Be back soon.'

Everything in place and taken care of to ensure I am able to progress with the business unencumbered Anthony reminded himself. He would stay in his flat from Monday to Friday while in London or even the odd weekend he may be required. Westwood House was back in the family and he would leave the Bentley for Sophie and buy something else for his use. Yes, it had turned out well overall he could continue to live his life as and when he wanted. At least Hugh would behave himself for the foreseeable future.

Beth, in a bathrobe opened the door to Anthony. He entered the room going straight to the dimly lit bedroom where he undressed hanging his suit and shirt in the wardrobe while Beth laid on the king size double bed propped up on her elbows watching him with erotic admiration. Naked he knelt in front of her slowly untying the bathrobe allowing it to fall open to expose her nakedness beneath. He controlled her eagerness and rising urgency, slowly stroking the soft sensuous skin of her thighs sending ripples of pleasure through her already anticipating body. Her mind clouded in ecstasy as she fought to control herself but she needed him so very much, it was almost painful as he worked his way up past her sensitive breasts to her neck kissing her tenderly until he found her red moist sensuous lips. Their gentle kiss pushed both over the edge exploding into desperate passion. He threw her roughly onto the bed where she was more than ready to receive him. She whimpered from another world as they worked each other using their mature experience to prolong the inevitable crescendos that were repeated over and over. He realised they hadn't said a word as they lay spent in each other's arms.

There was a knock on the door.

'Room service.' The dinner and champagne had arrived.

'Hello Mr Drax, so nice to see you.' Beth smiled as she uttered the first words of the evening. 'It was very kind of you to pay me a visit.'

'All in a days work Mrs Russell.'

Beth laughed.

They drank all of the champagne but ate little. Anthony left early morning before Beth was awake; he went back to his apartment to shower and change before going to the office.

The rest of the year fell into a steady routine with most weekends spent at Westwood House where he was able to continue his work while keeping the family happy. Emma was growing without difficulty and his mother and Sophie got on extremely well. The domestic staff helped greatly to take Sophie's mind off Anthony. Mrs Matthews paid regular visits and had developed a pleasant relationship with his mother. All was well, although Hugh still refused to visit Westwood House or attend any of the family functions. His deepening moodiness was both frustrating and unfathomable to the women.

The monthly London visits by Beth suited them both giving something they both needed outside their individual lives. They asked no more of each other.

Christmas came and went

It was in March the following year that David Russell was terminated from Harvey Engineering. Anthony had Harvey reluctantly fire the bullet. The repercussions were minimal except for David who folded into a drunken depression that resulted in him losing the other two accounts he held. He was broke, unemployed and abusive toward Beth. He berated her for not supporting him. Harvey her father for God's sake; it was her fault he was where he was. They had no relationship in or out of bed and damned if he was going to attend any of the Montague family functions. It went from bad to worse. David was having a sordid affair with a twenty eight year old drug addict whose husband tried to blackmail him ending up in a bloody pub brawl that had the whole town buzzing. Harvey arranged for the drug addict and her husband to move on and never darken Peterborough again. Beth moved in with her parents divorcing David and resuming the use of her maiden name. David Russell disappeared from Peterborough and it was reported that he had been seen somewhere in the Costa del Sol living in a dilapidated flat spending most days in the local bar babbling to those who would listen about the injustices that had befallen him. He was always filthy, smelling of vomit and urine, waking in some back alley most mornings to a blinding thirst. In time he faded from memory.

Beth Montague tried to convince Anthony that their assignations should be increased to twice a month but he persuaded her to stick with the arrangement they had, for the time being. He sensed she was becoming desperate and dependent on this one aspect of her life that provided some semblance of hope. He was tiring of her so needed to keep her at arms length although he did enjoy being able to use her at his convenience. He had taken her on several business trips but needed to be careful. She was controllable as long as he kept the reins on her. However, he would bring the next step of his long-term plan into play as soon as possible. It was all in the timing.

In September Sophie announced she was pregnant again, much to the delight of all and the indifference of Anthony. Sophie was happy and fully occupied with life at and around Westwood House. He thought it was early to have another child but it had its positives in that it would keep her and everyone else preoccupied.

It was March the following year when Simon Drax was born into the Westwood House world where he would flourish and develop into an upstanding young man. He inherited a high ability, ethics and morals, from his mother and grandmother on the Matthews side. He would eventually become a head boy at Allard Grammar much to the joy and pride of both families.

It was after Simon was born that Anthony reviewed his position. Maddison & Chapman had grown substantially and was increasingly recognised as one of the most prominent up and coming commercial accounting firms in London with subsidiaries in Manchester and Peterborough. Profits had soared with much of it being taken by Anthony as bonuses and dividends. With this and his takings from Harvey Engineering Anthony had paid the Westwood

House mortgage much earlier than planned. Banks were clamouring for his business with offers of most attractive loans. He was the man of the moment.

It was two days before Christmas when Harvey Montague was in London that Anthony invited him to a luncheon at the Lanes Park Hotel. Harvey was impressed, as Mr Drax was obviously well known by the staff hovering around him to meet his every request at a moments notice. Beth had left that morning for Peterborough. Harvey enjoyed a bottle of wine over dinner while Anthony stayed with his TG & T. Harvey didn't drink anything other than beer or wine. Anthony look directly at Harvey as they drank an after dinner coffee.

'I have a Christmas present for you Harvey.' Anthony handed him the plain sealed envelope.

'What have we here?' Harvey beamed and laughed reflecting his inebriated state. 'You're too kind and I must apologise as I can't reciprocate. I'll make it up to you.'

'You shouldn't worry Harvey although I'm sure you'll think of something.' Harvey smiled.

He eventually managed to open the envelope, withdrawing the sheaf of papers, placing them on the table in front of him. As he leafed through them a confused expression formed on his face through the wine mist. Slowly the implications of what he was reading dawned on him.

'Where did you get these from?' Harvey was sobering up fast.

'Don't worry, the originals are safe and sound.'

'I understood that Hugh had the originals?' He was still confused.

'He doesn't know I have them.' Anthony lied.

Cautiously and much more clearly Harvey looked at Anthony. Anthony didn't waver.

'Don't you think you should take everything to Hugh for safekeeping? These document are very dangerous Anthony so I suggest we take them to Hugh.'

Harvey wasn't getting it.

'Hugh doesn't know I have them and I won't burden my father in law with the knowledge that I have the originals.' Anthony lied again.

'Alright, I'll sort it out.'

'No Harvey, its time to think about what you are going to give me for Christmas.'

The game Anthony was playing was becoming clear to Harvey as the horror of it soaked into his mind. His anger rose with a primordial response to attack this bastard first and foremost on his mind. He was going to be blackmailed. He managed to control himself. After all, they were in the middle of a restaurant.

'What do you want?'

'You have been saying for some time you are tired and therefore looking forward to retirement. You will retire with immediate effect from Harvey Engineering. You will also gift all of your equity in Harvey Engineering to me. In return you will receive a lump sum payment of five hundred thousand pounds and retain you current salary until Harvey Engineering is sold or you die. It's a simple directive that you are in no position to question or refuse.'

Harvey winced, wishing he hadn't drunk so much wine as he couldn't think straight. If only he could talk to Hugh. There must be some way to counteract the situation he was in.

'Who would run Harvey Engineering?'

'Me.'

'But you don't have the ability or experience. Anthony, its not an easy position to be in.'

Anthony didn't respond but kept his steady unsmiling gaze on Harvey.

'I need to think about this and suggest we continue this discussion next week.'

Anthony placed a stock transfer form and agreement on the table in front of Harvey. He slowly reached into his coat pocket withdrawing his Mont Blanc pen placing it on the documents.

'No discussion, waiting or other delaying tactics, you have your home, investments, savings and your holiday house in Bordeaux with the very generous exit package I have allowed you, you will be very comfortable to say the least.' Anthony was measured in his response. 'You will sign the documents as the alternative won't be very palatable.'

Harvey thought about the proposal as Anthony spoke and while his hand was being forced, in a strange way it would be a relief to retire, leave it all behind and relax, watch the grass grow, spend time with family and friends. He decided, as Anthony had said the alternative was unthinkable. How could Hugh be so stupid as this matter would be hanging over their heads forever.

Harvey picked up the documents and read them through carefully until he was satisfied there were no rogue clauses. The devil is in the detail.

Without another word Harvey signed the documents, rose from the table and walked out of the restaurant.

Another enemy on the list!

Anthony took immediate control of Harvey Engineering much to the consternation of many of the staff, a minor problem that was quickly dispelled. The four senior managers were given more responsibilities with commensurate salary increases. All settled with business as usual returning within the week as the workload was impressive given the changes Anthony as finance director had introduce.

His meeting with the three senior staff of Maddison & Chapman took them by surprise. The offer was for a management buy out, which they in good faith accepted without hesitation. Harvey Engineering accounted for twenty five percent of the revenue that would remain into the foreseeable future as promised by Anthony. It took three months to complete the sale with the three new directors heavily committed to the agreed premium buy out price supplying personal guarantees for the loan used to pay out Anthony. Hugh retained his equity in the company, as he hadn't been consulted as to whether he wanted to sell or not. One month after the transaction had taken place and champagne corks had popped, Anthony gave Maddison & Chapman notice that he was withdrawing the Harvey Engineering account that was to be brought back in house. Thirty percent of the staff was dismissed and the heavily committed directors were plunged into hysterical depression. The enemy list grew while Anthony walked away a very wealthy cashed up man.

Anthony rented out his apartment in Kensington after purchasing outright a well-appointed new build apartment in Peterborough, only two blocks from where Beth Montague now lived. His asset base had decreased but cash holding massively increased. The extra commute on Friday and Monday to and from Westwood House wasn't inconvenient in the least as it gave time to think and plan the future of Harvey Engineering.

Beth was surprised that her father had suddenly and without explanation retired. She knew he was thinking about it but all the same such an instantaneous action was uncharacteristic. Then Anthony took over and moved in just down the road, which she had to admit, was convenient to say the least. Her monthly trips to London ceased although their liaison didn't. Anthony was aware of her relationship with the young Lord Montgomery Fortescue who lived at Nassington Hall on the edge of the ten thousand acre family estate. Lord Monty was besotted with Beth who found him a bit of a bore but he was free with his money and well connected. Her social life suited her well, keeping her entertained. It was only when her father told her reluctantly that the generous allowance she had always received would be no more that she seriously looked at her options including the many marriage proposals from Monty. Beth acted quickly and decisively so Monty and Beth had a lavish wedding at Nassington Hall on a clear sunny day in August. Anthony was unconcerned about the marriage although he did agree to see Beth fortnightly rather than monthly, it broke the monotony of living alone.

It was on the Tuesday morning when he received the call. Summer had come with a vengeance that year with its hot shimmering heat drying out the hardiest of waterways causing national water restrictions to save the dwindling reservoir supplies especially throughout the southern regions. London was sweltering, people died, as did his mother. The call was from Sophie breaking the news to which he responded in a matter of fact manner. He travelled to Westwood to make the necessary arrangements, staying over until the funeral, a low-key affair with the usual inane church service complete with religious platitudes and tired out-dated ceremony. Only Anthony, Sophie, the two children and Mrs Matthews attended. As usual Hugh was indisposed much to the annoyance of Sophie. Once the funeral was over Anthony returned to Peterborough. When he had gone Sophie reflected on having him home for well over a week. She knew they had grown apart and was saddened by how much. What is to become of them was the question Sophie asked herself, but deep down she suspected the worst. Anthony didn't show his frustration at the inconvenience he felt over the death and funeral although there was some recognition that an era was over, he was suddenly an orphan. When he returned to Peterborough he was back to the routine of work, home and Beth. The visits to home became infrequent. The years drifted by and the enemy list grew. His belligerent attitude at Harvey Engineering continued to get people offside with a higher than industry standard resignations and disruptions that were beginning to tell on the performance of the company.

His drinking had become problematic, a reflection of his boredom and frustration.

8

'Good evening Anthony, another busy week?' Toby Thornton was the publican at the White Swan, walking distance from Anthony's apartment. Anthony had a meeting in the morning and wouldn't be going to Westwood.

'Same as last week Toby.' It was Friday evening and Anthony sat on his usual stool at the bar and ordered a pint of Farcet Mill bitter, a regional beer produced by Ortan Brewery on the outskirts of Peterborough. Built in the eighteenth century it didn't produce much else than this regional and much loved beer.

'I heard through the grapevine that you lost your senior workshop manager.'

'The grapevine was right Toby.' Anthony offered no explanation.

'How is business in the White Swan Toby?'

'Not bad at all actually.' Toby lied. He was just keeping his head above water. The pub should be heaving but it was only half full as was the case every Friday night with Saturday often being worse.

'I have a small stake in the Ortan Brewery you know, an investment I made years ago. I sit on the board, a bit of a token position to make up the numbers I suspect.'

'Who owns the brewery?' Anthony wasn't really interested.

'The Fortescue family own it. One of the many acquisitions over the years although they weren't interested in it as Lord Fortescue rarely attends board meetings. Between you and me the brewery isn't doing well and they are considering selling.'

So, Elizabeth Fortescue has married into a brewery, thought Anthony.

Just as Toby started to pull a beer there was a tap on his shoulder.

'Hello Anthony.' He turned to see Bradley Smith, the president of the local chamber of commerce.

'Bradley.'

'There are a few friends having a drink over near the fireplace. Would you like to join us?'

'Very kind of you Bradley.' Anthony stood and with beer in hand to follow Bradley to where a small group sat deep in conversation. He knew everyone there.'

'Hello Anthony.' They chorused.

'Hello all.' Anthony pulled up a chair.

For the next hour they chattered about the politics of business in the area with Anthony making little comment. He was seen as a very important businessman in the area having taken over from Harvey Montague including the membership of the chamber. He had even been appointed to a working committee on the future development of business in the area. Anthony thought the committee was too idealistic and out of touch to have any effect. But it killed some time.

'Anthony, several of us are having a dinner tomorrow evening at the Hyde Club and thought you may like to join us?'

'Any particular agenda?' A business dinner is even worst than a drink in the pub with this lot, he groaned to himself.

'Very much a social evening, no business I assure you.' Bradley laughed.

Anthony wondered if he had read his mind.

'In that case I accept.' Beats sitting in on my own he said to himself.

'OK see you there at seven thirty in the bar for pre-dinner drinks.'

'Goodnight Bradley.'

The Hyde Club was the closest thing to a five star restaurant. Food was excellent and the ambiance impressive. The few times Anthony had been there in the early days had impressed and made it a must venue for any important business dinners.

Anthony arrived by taxi at seven forty joining the seven people already sitting at a table in the bar. Introductions were made and out of the seven people he only knew two, Bradley and his wife Joan. The others were partners with one single woman, Sue Hetherington, wife of Samuel Hetherington a successful old family farmer who specialised in cattle breading. Samuel was at a cattle-breeding conference for a week. He ate, drank and dreamed cattle breeding.

Conversation was pleasant and intelligent with spates of quiet laughter that seemed very relaxing. Anthony hadn't been in such company for a long time.

Sue and Anthony were seated together.

'So you're the Mr Drax of Harvey Engineering.' Sue Hetherington was not vivacious but rather a bright intelligent personality that Anthony had been observing during drinks.

'The very same, Mrs Hetherington.' Anthony smiled.

'Sue, please.'
'It has to be Anthony then.'
Orders were taken and drinks refreshed. They chattered while waiting for their meals finding they had similar interests and opinions. They were comfortable with each other. Sue was pleased she had been seated with someone who looked smart in his dinner suit, knew how to behave and didn't know anything about cattle or their breeding.
The evening finished at a respectable hour and while the couples wandered out to the car park, Anthony walked towards the entrance.
'I need to order a taxi.' Sue walked towards to reception.
'Hold on Sue, I have a car coming so you might as well take it after he drops me off.'
'You sure Anthony?'
'It's on the company account. Here it comes now.'
Anthony opened the back door for Sue. Sue looked around the Mercedes that was obviously top of the range.
'Evening Mr Drax.'
'Good evening David.'
David drove down the driveway from the club.
'Is this your company car?' Sue couldn't see any taxi identification.
'No it's David's car, we have a private arrangement which is very convenient as he is always available.' Sue looked out of the window into the dark cold night illuminated by the street lamp centauries running as the car passed, they neared Anthony's Apartment.
'Penny for your thoughts.'
Sue turned and looked at Anthony.

'I was just thinking what a pleasant evening it has been. It has been a long time since I've had a relaxed calm dinner without the usual boisterous nonsense of one-upmanship and innuendo.'

'Very pleasant indeed Sue, hopefully we can do it again in the not too distant future.' David stopped the car outside Anthony's apartment.

'Well, I'll leave you in David's capable hands.' Anthony opened the car door and got out, turned and leaned towards Sue.

'Goodnight Sue and hopefully catch up soon.'

'Goodnight Anthony and thank you again, it's very considerate of you.'

Anthony watched until the car had driven out of sight contemplating the fact that no exchange of numbers or confirmation of getting together had taken place. Oh well, maybe nothing will come of it. He decided not to pursue her as the ball is now in her court, although the thought of bedding her was attractive. We'll see.

When the telephone rang Anthony was reviewing the monthly management accounts with a view to increase the profit margin which he would divert into his own pocket to keep the company taxable profit minimal or even a small loss would be better.

'Anthony Drax.'

'Hello Anthony, its Sue Hetherington.'

'Sue, what a pleasant surprise, what do I owe the pleasure?' Anthony hadn't given Sue much thought after their evening out.

'We have a charity event coming up next month and I was hoping you would attend as there is an auction for fundraising so we need to invite as many people as possible. All very much for a good cause of course and I can assure you of a pleasant evening.'

'So, I'm only useful for an auction?' laughed Anthony.

'I didn't mean it like that Anthony' Sue was careful and non-apologetic 'It's a black tie evening with a three course meal, meet and greet and dancing, so overall it should be a great evening.'

'I appreciate the invitation Sue but I don't do this sort of event as I am on my own here and its something my wife isn't interested in.'

'Don't worry about being on your own Anthony as I can assure you, you won't be.' So Samuel is going to be at one of his cattle breeding seminars thought Anthony.

'All taken care of and please say you will come.' Sue was persistent.

'Seems like an offer too good to refuse Sue. Perhaps we could meet up beforehand and you can tell me more about the charity and the evening?'

'Well, actually I thought the same, however, the best person for you to meet would be Julie Ford the charity's PR director. She's a delight Anthony and I am sure you two will get on very well. Anyway, I'll be at the evening so it will be good to catch up with you then.' She had played all her cards.

Anthony hesitated, what was this about, she gives me the come on and then brushes me off. He wondered if he had read her wrong.

'Not necessary Sue, let's just leave it and we can catch up at the function.' He was put out, even miffed. As if he was going to be played.

'Too late I'm afraid as I have already arranged for Julie to call you to make arrangements. Be a darling and give her an opportunity, please?'

Sue sitting at her desk contemplated what had transpired between them and thought it would have been so easy to fall into a relationship with Anthony that would have brought some excitement to her dull and boring life she shared with the antithesis of Anthony Drax. It wasn't that she didn't care for Samuel it was just that he was so predictable and could be ridiculously crass at times. But life with him was very comfortable though, as he provided well including a very generous allowance, no questions asked, so very much a free agent. Anthony was obviously well heeled but then there were the rumours surrounding Anthony that regularly cropped up in conversation and always seemed to find its way into the gossip. His ruthless business tactics and general derogatory attitude towards his employees were well substantiated. To say he was not well liked by those involved directly with him was an understatement. The contradiction was that he is charming to women although she suspected all women were just fair game to be conquered and discarded. His generosity to charities was calculated, designed for his benefit. Those who did not have business dealings or were not close to him found it difficult to reconcile the rumours so didn't. The local government funded organisations would seek out his advice and support as a presentable and successful businessman who splashed the cash, drove the best car and travelled regularly much to their envy. Little did they understand that he was not a good businessman but gained his financial success at the expense of others, his path littered with people made destitute with careers destroyed, trying desperately to support their suffering families. He was somewhat aware of the suffering and pain he inflicted but in silent consciousness took a perverse pleasure in being able to inflict such torment. No, Sue decided that it was not an option to get involved with this smiling assassin, as he was referred to, even with his charm and attraction, fatal attraction really. Also his drinking was legendry to boot, as it was reported when he was with male company he needed to drink each and everyone under the table to show his superiority, he had to be the alpha male. God knows what he was doing to his body that he worked hard to maintain in reasonable condition.

Julie Ford called exactly ten minutes after Sue had hung up.

'Hello Mr Drax, I'm Julie Ford. Sue Hetherington asked me to call to make a suitable time to meet with you. What would be the best time?'

Her voice was professional, silky, almost seductive but to the point. No doubt about it, thought Anthony, always get a woman to do the PR, which in this case was definitely more of a sales function. Although, initially adamant that he would turn her down as a rebuff to Sue for her manipulative tactics the voice changed his mind. Let's see if the person attached to the voice was as seductive.

'Six thirty at the Hyde Club, I'll see you in the bar.'

'Perfect Mr Drax, I look forward to meeting you. Six thirty then, take care and thank you for giving me your time.'

The early cold darkness of winter had well and truly enveloped the Hyde Club by the time Anthony drove into the car park. Although it was a perfectly still evening, as he walked towards the welcoming lights, the promises of warmth that engulfed him as he entered reception. He checked his coat and scarf before making sure he was all in order, as he had come straight from the office. In the foyer mirror he noticed the five o'clock shadow added to his image. Popping a mint into his mouth he walked into the bar noting the two men at the bar were the sole occupants. He sat on one of the nest of four comfortable lounge chairs in the softly lit corner to the right of the entrance fully aware that when people entered such a place they always looked to their left first scanning the room to the right which would give him time to check her out without her noticing. It was six fifteen.
'Would you like anything to drink Mr Drax?' The drinks waiter hovered expressionless.
'A pint of Farcet Mill.' Known in the local vernacular as 'the Mill' it was a reasonable beer. Anthony wondered what was happening with the Ortan Brewery and made a mental note to catch up with Toby Thornton.
'I am waiting for someone and when she comes in can you come over immediately to take her order.'
'Yes Mr Drax.'
Several couples and suited businessmen had come in and settled for after work drinks at the bar.
At exactly six thirty a woman entered the bar, stood and looked to her left slowly scanning the room to her right. At a slim five foot five with shoulder length hair the well-cut business suit augmented her attractive figure. She slowly

walked towards the bar searching for Anthony. He was impressed at the sensual unconscious sway of her hips even though she held herself erect with her left arm slightly bent at the elbow, then without warning she turned to her right and looked directly at him. About thirty-five Anthony guessed. When their eyes met a soft smile lit her rather beautiful elf like face and she walked directly towards Anthony who rose as she approached.

'Mr Drax.' She extended her hand.

'Julie Ford I presume.' Anthony smiled as he took her warm soft hand. She squeezed his hand firmly, to which he responded holding for a moment longer than normally was the custom. Her perfume, like her was soft and sensual without being overpowering.

'Have a seat Julie and call me Anthony please.' She sat opposite him, in the furthest possible seat possible and crossed her shapely legs. Very nice indeed he thought.

'Can I take your order?' The expressionless waiter was back.

'I'll have a G & T, no ice with a twist of lime please.' Julie gave her order to the waiter.

'I'm fine thank you.' Anthony had barely touched the Fawcett Mill.

'Yes Mr Drax.'

The waiter moved towards the bar.

'Well now Julie, Sue tells me you're best suited to give me an overview of what the upcoming function is all about.'

Julie launched into the charity's standard spiel to which Anthony didn't listen but concentrated on the woman herself. Julie was acutely aware of what Anthony was doing so kept the brief to a minimum. Conversation lapsed into anything but work, which was comfortable for both. After their next round of drinks Anthony invited Julie to stay for dinner if she didn't have any prior arrangements.

'That's very kind of you Anthony, nothing planned as only my cat Misty is at home waiting for me.' She purposely made the point.

'No Mr Ford then?' Anthony asked

'Ford is my maiden name. Until December last year I was Mrs Julie Taylor, since then I have been enjoying my independence, more so my freedom. After the divorce I moved from Norwich to take up this position. A new job and life that has been everything I was hoping for' Julie chuckled softly. Julie talked directly looking into his eyes which rather than being disconcerting Anthony found it an attractive characteristic of this interesting woman.

'Children?'

'No, even though we were married for ten years without precaution nothing happened. In retrospect, although I am definitely not adverse to children it was probably for the best. Who knows what the future brings.'

'Excuse me Julie.' Anthony rose and walked towards the toilets aware of being watched by Julie.

As he walked Julie looked with appreciation at this very wealthy man as he cut a fine figure although with a hint of midriff thickening. She had left her past behind and at thirty-six knew she had to make a move sooner than later to establish herself in a relationship that would bring her the lifestyle she wanted. No getting involved with anyone who didn't have the money and resources to allow her to live an affluent life. She had been Mrs average before and it was not going to happen again. Julie knew that she had been blessed with a firm attractive body that she looked after plus a developed sophisticated demeanour that was appreciated and allowed her to be accepted into the higher circles of society. She never threatened other women by flirting with their husbands or giving any reason to undermine their trust in her. Julie was articulate and intelligent, trusted by all women and desired by all men. She smiled to herself, a perfect wife for the ruthless Mr Drax, except he's married.

The Mercedes pulled up as Anthony and Julie walked down the steps from the Hyde Club. The meal had been excellent and conversation pleasant. Anthony dwelt on his business successes and the lifestyle this provides for him, in detail. Julie wrongfully thought that he had an ego problem whereas it was more his narcissistic personality that she would soon discover. She listened patiently asking loaded questions that would further massage his need to demonstrate his achievements. It was surprising just how transparently simple Anthony is she thought, but he needed to be handled carefully if she was to achieve the end result. Yes, he will do very nicely thank you she thought.

'Mr Drax.'

'Hello David.' Anthony didn't introduce Julie.

The Mercedes drove towards Anthony's apartment.

Julie placed her hand gently on Anthony's arm as they chattered about the arrangements for the forthcoming charity function. For Anthony her hand felt comfortable and friendly although it didn't dampen his desire to conquer this beautiful and interesting woman at the first possible opportunity.

The Mercedes pulled up outside the apartment. Anthony turned to Julie.

'Would you like to come in for a nightcap?'

'Not tonight Anthony as busy day tomorrow and one too many glasses of wine I'm afraid' she touched his arm again 'thank you for a lovely evening, you don't know how much I appreciate it and hopefully I'll see you soon. Goodnight.'

'It was a pleasure Julie and I guarantee we will do this again very soon.'

Anthony got out of the car and lent in the door.

'Miss Ford will give you directions David.'

'That's fine Mr Drax, goodnight.'

Anthony looked at Julie and she gave him a final sensuous sultry smile.

'Pity you weren't coming in for a nightcap.' Anthony chuckled giving her a wink before standing up to close the door.

'Anthony' called Julie 'by the way, I'll be your partner at the charity function. I'm looking forward to it, goodnight.'

'A pleasant surprise Julie, goodnight.' The door closed and the Mercedes drove off.

Anthony walked to the front door thinking that at least she could have come in and shown her appreciation in an appropriate manner. He smiled to himself, next time.

Julie sat back into the rear plush leather seat and reflected on the evening that had gone very well in presenting an unexpected sea change for her life. It is fait accompli for you Mr Drax and you will have to wait to savour the sweet fruits of this girl don't you worry about that. You may think you have caught the marlin my boy but you have to land it first. Julie laughed out loud. David looked at her in the rear vision mirror wondering what could be so funny but daren't ask.

As he expected, the charity function was predictable in format, food and company. Julie insisted that they meet at the venue, the town hall with its cavernous ballroom having been tastefully decorated with a multitude of round tables covered in pristine white ironed table cloths on which the silver cutlery sat to attention along side the ornate council placemats surrounded by a champagne flute, red and white wine glasses and a water glass with the water jugs already in place. Bottles of wine had been corked and place strategically around the table complimenting the arrangement of fresh flowers emitting their bouquet softly throughout.

Julie watched Anthony as he surveyed all, letting him stand for a few minutes before going to meet him, as it was not her intention to give him the impression that she was eager for his company. He was stunning in his tuxedo that was obviously bespoke; a perfect cut that augmented his well-groomed look and handsome features. By the time she walked from the other side of the room to Anthony, several people had approached him with the men shaking his hand and the women giving a warm hug with the traditional light kiss on the cheek.

She stopped half way to greet some guests, acutely aware that he had seen her and was watching intently.

Anthony had spotted Julie as soon as he had walked into the ballroom but feigned ignorance. Her emerald green cocktail dress did everything it was supposed to do, as she had planned. It contrasted her pale skin, green eyes and black hair to maximum understated effect ensuring she didn't upstage the other women but attracted the admiration of the men, portrayed by their side glances. He watched her walking across the ballroom floor towards him as she smiled warmly at the women, passing comments and swapping subtle laughter. She paid little attention to their men. Very clever he thought.

'Hello Anthony ' Julie lent up and gave him a welcoming peck on the cheek 'well, don't you look smart. Ready for an enjoyable evening?'

'As I said before, not really my thing but with a beautiful girl at my side on the Mayor's table it can't be anything but enjoyable, what would you like to drink?'

'I'll wait for dinner so the question is what would you like to drink?' she teased.

'A beer would be a good starter.' Anthony looked around.

'The bar is at the back of the ballroom, come on.' She took his arm as they made their way through the tables where people were already sitting while others searched for their place cards. They made a handsome couple that didn't go unnoticed by her friends and many other women. If there were any undisclosed concerns they were dispelled, as they were safe with her having a partner. The men were envious.

They were seated at the Lord Mayor's table with several old family business cohorts who expected nothing else. For Anthony it massaged his ego to be seen seated at the mayor's table. His advantage was that he was handsome, well groomed and quite slim contrasted against the old moneyed fat, squidgy locals who hadn't contributed to their wealth but rode on the coat tails of their ancestors.

Anthony felt superior. Much of the discussion was about local politics that bored him to tears.

It was the seating strategy that Julie skilfully managed while remaining in the background neither wanting or receiving credit from Anthony who was incapable of giving credit even if he realised it was due.

With the meal completed, wine drank and spirits high, the auction began in earnest. A long past sports celebrity from London had been engaged as the master of ceremonies for the evening with the task of also being the auctioneer. Slightly inebriated, he subjected the gathering to a string of tired jokes and out-dated stories from his sporting experiences with outrageous transparent embellishment that caused most of the laughter and a considerable number of audible groans. You get what you pay for. Auction items progressively sold on the crash of the gavel without any involvement from Anthony until the last highlight item of the evening, a four day weekend at the Marbella Club Hotel including first class return flights and an ample expense account with the only proviso that it had to be taken in two weeks time. The bidding started in a frenzy of drunken excitement with the bid price quickly rising to an eye watering level.

'The last bid rests with you Mr Hetherington. Do we have anymore bids.' The auctioneer raised his gavel to the audience who excitedly looked around the ballroom in anticipation. Calls and yelps rained over the room.

'For the first time I am going to sell.' Deathly silence fell over the crowd. 'For the second time I am going to sell.' The silence was palpable. 'For the third time.' Anthony Drax raised his hand. 'Yes Mr Drax?' The auctioneer pointed his gavel at Anthony upon whom all eyes were fixed.

Firmly and calmly Anthony rose looking straight at the auctioneer 'I'll double the last bid.' The pregnant pause preceded a loud unison gasp that vibrated throughout the crowd. The auctioneer looked confused through a veil of alcohol but quickly regained his composure and looked straight at Samuel Hetherington.

'For the first, second and third time I will sell.' The auctioneer waved his gavel hysterically in the air. 'Sold' He screamed as the gavel came crashing down, drowned out by a cacophony of cheers, screams and clapping that rolled throughout the large ballroom for more than a minute or two. Never in the twenty-five year history of the charity had such a dramatic end to an auction been witnessed with a fundraising total setting a record that would never be surpassed, as Anthony or Samuel Hetherington would never bid again at the charity auction. Although he had paid three times the value of the Marbella Club Hotel package, Anthony had cemented his place in the community as a philanthropist of considerable wealth who more importantly had put Samuel Hetherington in his place once and for all, much to the joy of many in the grand ballroom, including the Mayor.

Samuel sat ashen faced trying to comprehend what had just taken place. For the past fifteen years he had outbid everyone on the final prestigious auction item, he was noted for it and expected it. Winning the auction was integral to his standing in the community, his ego and his existence and now, that bastard Drax had stolen it from him. Waves of self inflicted humiliation passed over him as for the first time in many years he couldn't wallow in the sycophantic 'hail fellow well met' and back slapping of congratulations. Sue laughed inwardly at the turn of events as now, maybe, this would humble Samuel somewhat. At least she wouldn't have to put with his self-aggrandizement but it was annoying that she would miss out on the Marbella trip that she had started packing for. That's what you get for backing the wrong horse. Nobody was paying attention to Samuel, as focus centred on Anthony as the night moved on to more important things such as dancing and drinking that swept Anthony along with it, well at least the drinking.

'Well done Mr Drax.' Julie congratulated Anthony on his auction win as they walked down the steps to towards David waiting in his Mercedes.

'Served a purpose actually Julie. However, I'll endeavour to enjoy myself.'

Julie lent her back against the car as Anthony embraced her with obvious intent. She let him take the initiative. He kissed her softly as their bodies pressed firmly together, slightly marred by the smell of alcohol. Julie was surprised at the volume he could consume with seemingly little effect although she doubted if he could get it up tonight. Although, surprisingly his passion for Julie became very obvious as their kiss lingered pleasantly. Not tonight Mr Drax.

'Are you available to come back for a nightcap.' Anthony asked. She put her arms around his neck and pulled him firmly into her body.

'Unfortunately I need to assist the team with sorting out bits and pieces ready for the clean up crew coming in the morning. Perhaps Wednesday after work we can catch up?' Julie kissed him softly.

'Alright then.' Anthony hid his disappointment. They stepped back and he opened the car door.

'Julie, could you do something for me please?'

'Of course Anthony, what is it?'

'Extend the four night stay at the Marbella Club Hotel to seven nights and upgrade to a grand villa. Get their account details and I'll do a bank transfer.'

'That sounds very exotic Mr Drax. First thing in the morning if that's alright with you?' So far so good, Julie smiled sweetly mocking subservience.

'It would be a waste not to take someone with me so I suggest you put in for eight days leave and accompany me?'

'Strictly business I presume?'

'Strictly business Miss Ford, goodnight Julie, I'll hear from you in the morning. Thank you for your support as I have a busy week but look forward to catching up Wednesday.' The Mercedes pulled away before Julie could respond. Anthony sat back reflecting on his evening that had turned out remarkably well. It's amazing how the unexpected happens when you are least expecting it. He chuckled at his own pun and was happy at the prospect of having the elusive Julie to himself.

Julie watched the car pull away. It's amazing how the unexpected happens when you plan for it. She smiled to herself as she walked back into the hall planning to keep him at arms length until the trip.

❖

The Marbella Club Hotel private limousine pulled quietly up to the tastefully designed Spanish square pillared entrance where their dedicated concierge waited. Nicolás Rodríguez opened the car door for Julie and introduced himself then escorted them to the villa followed by the porter with the their cases and bags.

'Mr Drax and Miss Ford, would you come with me please while Isabella unpacks your cases?' Nicolás led them to a secluded area in the Terrace Bar where warm face towels and iced spring water with a twist of lemon waited for them. A waiter hovered behind Nicolás.

'I will leave you in the capable hands of Matías while I check to see all is in order at your villa. I am sure Isabella will be finished shortly. Please relax after your journey.' Nicolás quickly walked away being replaced by the immaculately dressed Matías splendid in his high-necked white coat and black trousers down to his patent leather shoes. This swarthy young Spaniard was impressive to the eye Julie reflected.

'Would you like anything to drink or eat señor, señorita?' Matías looked at Julie ignoring Anthony.

'I'll have a Sau Sau thank you Matías.' Anthony raised his eyebrows. He had never heard of a Sau Sau and wondered if Julie had been here before or had she had just done her research. Julie always did her research but more detailed in this instance.

'Mahou Cinco Estrella, por favor' Anthony wouldn't risk deviating to a Sau Sau or dare show his ignorance. Matías retreated to the bar while they refreshed with the face towels and relaxed in the cool quiet garden surround. It had been a busy morning.

163

'This is very pleasant.' Julie closed her eyes feeling the stress and tiredness drain from her body, so nice to be away from the routine and depressing weather.

The luxury villa was cool and pristine, very modern while retaining its Spanish heritage impressing them as they entered. Their clothes had been unpacked so that Julie had to rummage through several draws before she found her brief black bikini.

'Time for a swim Anthony before we dress for dinner.' Anthony wasn't used to being ordered around but decided to go with the flow. Actually he had never been with such a beautiful strong willed woman such as Julie, a new and very different experience. Normally women were intimidated by his manner and wealth, not Julie who was very much her own person. Anthony quite liked the change and challenge, especially the prospect of seducing such a wild card or being seduced, which he hoped was more the case.

'Sounds like a plan Julie, I'll get my bathers.' As he turned to the bedside draw Julie pulled her white cotton dress over her head and threw it on the bed, leaving her in her white brief lace panties and bra. He turned to see her unfasten her bra letting it drop to the floor exposing her modest but perfectly formed white breasts accentuated by light brown areola. She slipped her panties down her beautiful firm legs to stand in front of him unashamedly naked with her black hair matched by her pubic region. She was breathtaking, not a picking on her and as firm as an athlete without having severe muscular delineation. Anthony was aroused by not only this naked form in front of him that he hadn't had the pleasure of enjoying but also the relaxed confident attitude she had with her nudity. He liked what he saw and for the first time thought there could be more to a relationship with this woman. Julie picked up her bikini and started dressing.

'Come on Mr, stop ogling and get your bathers on. If you're a good boy you may be in for a treat this evening.' Anthony laughed out loud unaware that Julie was playing him at his own game.

'Well it could very well be my lucky day then.' Anthony started to take off his cream linen suit.

'I'll see you down by the pool.' Julie had put her white beach shift over her bikini-clad beauty complimenting her Saint Laurent sandals and Pia Rossini broad rimmed hat. She turned to Anthony giving him a seductive smile. 'Don't be long as you never know how many Spanish boys there could be at the pool.' She teased. He watched her walk out of the bedroom with accentuated swinging hips to obviously tease him further. She knows how to dress for a charity worker he thought. Obviously been on expensive holidays before.

Undressed, Anthony looked at himself in the full-length mirror showing his well-formed strong body. He frowned at his thickening mid section, a result of too much beer and poor diet he surmised. Need to do something about that.

They relaxed by and in the pool enjoying the exclusive setting with several other couples discretely dotted around. The sangria was the best he had tasted which was to be expected in such a prestigious hotel known for its history of catering to the celebrities of the world. They fell into a comfortable relaxed afternoon of chatter about everything and nothing, which was refreshing for Anthony

as it gave him a new perspective of what the future could hold as he looked at and shared his time with this woman.
Anthony pushed Sophie and the children to the furthest reaches of his mind. He had been due a home visit but the 'business trip' to Spain changed his plans. His estranged relationship with Sophie was difficult, so his time was spent with the children or working while at Westwood House that now held little sentimental value and the trip down and back to Teddington was tedious to say the least. It was not his life. The saving grace was the children, especially Simon his son, although much different to Anthony, nevertheless his son, and they got on well. More like his mother's nature with a spark from his father Anthony thought. Like most sons Simon looked up to his father.
They had dressed for dinner and were now enjoying the nouvelle cuisine prepared by the Michelin Star chef famous for his seafood creations that drew many of the guests from around the world to the art deco Champagne Room. Julie's plan for the evening required that Anthony drank little so she ordered a bottle of Billecart-Salmon making it last throughout the meal by creating a conversation laced with subtle innuendo calculating that he would comply in anticipation. Anthony of course unwittingly complied in anticipation of what was to come as he had invested much in this woman who he found intriguing if not slightly dominating, an experience he wasn't used to. There was no doubt that Julie was a force to be reckoned with, beautiful and alluring she definitely was. Someone he felt comfortable with and pleased to have on his arm, drawing attention and admiration from the other guests.

Julie didn't disappoint. She took the initiative that evening to which Anthony willingly succumbed. Her lovemaking was strong and direct, leaving him with little to think about except to enjoy the experience something he did for the remainder of their stay. They made love, slept, swam, relaxed and enjoyed the fine dining. It was three months later over breakfast in Anthony's apartment that Julie quietly shared that she was pregnant and on the fourth month Anthony told Sophie that he wanted a divorce.

9

Simon Drax graduated from university in mechanical and process engineering without distinction but it was a solid degree. His work experience had been at Harvey Engineering on the shop floor under the guidance of the works manager Malcolm Henning. Malcolm, a methodical and precise engineer with some thirty years experience took Simon under his wing without comment or prejudice against the son of the boss although Simon received his fair share of side comments from the workmen who initially viewed him with some suspicion. However he soon proved to be the antithesis of his arrogant and aloof father strutting around the shop floor on an irregular basis. On graduation he moved into a small flat near the engineering works opting to stay out of Anthony's life although Anthony had made a reluctant offer to have Simon reside with him. Simon purposely developed his own lifestyle and friends outside arms reach of Anthony. They met for breakfast every Friday morning at the newly refurbished Café The Ferry. He spent most weekends at Westwood House with his mother and sister.

Over time Simon earned the respect of his fellow workers on the shop floor and had been noticed management. He proved to be intelligent, studious and diligent, quickly becoming a respected member of the team working his way through the ranks to junior management.

Simon and Anthony quickly became known as "chalk" and "cheese" in Harvey Engineering as Simon's friendly personality and hard work was appreciated. He learnt early that respect was earned something his father had no concept of.

For Simon the announcement of the divorce of his parents was not unexpected, deep down he knew it was inevitable. His mother also knew it was inevitable but supressed such thoughts and feelings. Still, she would find it difficult with the pain such partings conjured up. Anthony had emotionally and physically left long ago. His life had developed into something else.

'Mr Drax is here for his two pm meeting Mr Matthews.'

'Show him into my private meeting room please Miss Blair.' Hugh knew exactly why Anthony Drax had made the appointment with him at the Matthews, Fortescue & Miller offices. There had been some preliminary discussions between Anthony and Sophie over the terms of the pending divorce, with Anthony being of the opinion that Sophie had brought nothing to the marriage and therefore should leave with nothing. Any feeling he had for Sophie had dissipated long ago without the concept or appreciation that she had given him two children and brought them up to be sensible and well adjusted. His argument was that he had financed the development of his children so all was equal. He discounted the fact that Sophie had foregone her own legal career in caring for the children so her earning ability was much depreciated. Anyhow, the Matthews family was well heeled so why should he be responsible in anyway shape or form. They were at a stalemate something Anthony needed to be resolved as soon as possible so he could wed Julie Ford, the mother of his next child and someone who could offer a new and invigorated life.

The ace Anthony had up his sleeve was the hold he had over Hugh he used effectively in acquiring Maddison & Chapman. He still held the damning documents signed by all three of the perpetrators. Something Hugh was well aware of but the tide had turned.

'Anthony.' Hugh walked confidentially into the oak paneled meeting room where Anthony sat reading the Financial Times.

'Hugh.' Anthony responded without getting up.

'What brings you here?' Both Hugh and Anthony knew very well what the agenda was.

Unsmiling, Anthony looked Hugh straight in the eyes.

'You know very well why I am here Hugh. You will need to sort your daughter out and get her to sign the divorce agreement prepared by my solicitor.' Anthony was impatient.

Hugh looked old and tired but very much at home in his office. He poured himself a coffee from the silver urn, no milk or sugar, walked to his mahogany desk with green leather inlay framed by a polished brass border. The coaster upon which he placed the coffee cup was one of a set of twelve he had received from King George VI immediately after the end of the war, in recognition of the company's contribution to the war effort. Hugh was proud of the reputation of Matthews, Fortescue & Miller that he had sullied by his involvement with Henry Drax and Harvey Simpson. How could he have been so stupid? It was time to put the matter to bed.

'Anthony' Hugh looked at his estranged supercilious son in law 'there will be no signing of the agreement you provided as the condition of your divorce from Sophie.

The divorce will be dealt with by the court.' Hugh sat back into his high back leather office chair that complimented not only the mahogany desk but also the office overall.

'You seem to have forgotten the understanding we have in regard to certain criminal activities you were involved with.' Anthony spat out as his anger flared. How dare this jumped up solicitor tell me what will or won't be signed. The red mist descended.

Hugh sighed and arose from his chair.

'Excuse me for a minute Anthony, I will be right back.' Hugh walked to a side door in the office that led into an adjoining room. Anthony was slightly defused at this but didn't respond. He heard voices from the adjoining room and was suddenly overcome with uncertainty as the shiver ran from the base of his spine over his body. Something he hadn't experienced since his mother sat him down to explain that his father had left them and they needed to move out of Westwood House.

The door opened and Hugh came back into the office carrying a large pile of files followed by Harvey Montague carrying several reels of recording tape.

Anthony felt intimidated and astounded at this turn of events, as he hadn't expected anyone else to be involved, especially Harvey. As far as Anthony was concerned he had kept Hugh and Harvey separated over their activities. Obviously he had been naive to think they wouldn't discuss his involvement, obviously conspiring against him.

Anthony jumped to his feet 'Look here, what's this about? What is Harvey doing here? This is nothing to do with him Hugh.' Anthony was confused and threatened.

'Sit down Anthony.' Barked Hugh. Harvey said nothing but looked strangely confident which added to Anthony's discomfort. He sat back down.

'Now, you will listen to me Anthony without interjection or disruption. When I have finished you will be invited to make comment.' The authority and sternness Hugh spoke with was something Anthony hadn't experienced before. The thunderous look on his face told Hugh and Harvey he was yet to be tamed. Very shortly thought Hugh.

'You stole a private document that related to an agreement between myself, Harvey and your father and according to law, if you had concerns that it was illegal, you should have lodged it with the public prosecutor leaving the matter to take its own course. Instead, you decided to use this information to blackmail both Harvey and myself. Your father took the option to move to Spain with his secretary where he now resides in comfort on the proceeds of the transaction mentioned in the document. Your terms of the blackmail were to effectively steal Maddison & Chapman and Harvey Engineering. We understand you didn't impose any terms upon your father so can only assume you are protecting him from any action.'

Anthony rose aggressively from his seat. 'I have no interest in or desire to see my father.' Interjected Anthony. 'I haven't a clue where he is and don't care as he is the furthest thing from my mind. I am not interested in what you are saying Hugh ... '

'I can assure you, you will be Anthony' Hugh cut him off 'and you can have your say later. Now sit down and be quiet while I finish telling you how things are going to be from now on.' Anthony sat down, his demeanor changing from the aggressor to the confused wounded. Typical behaviour of a coward thought Hugh.

Hugh and Harvey held Anthony with their steady gazes as Hugh continued.

'I'll cut to the chase. By your action of blackmail you are in collusion with any illegal activities you have construed from the agreement you stole. Furthermore, what you have done is no doubt extortion which in itself is a criminal offence, so in effect your position is far more precarious than either of myself or Harvey's if it was to be investigated.' Harvey's eyes drilled into Anthony making him uncomfortable.

'Most conversations' Hugh continued 'you had with myself and Harvey were recorded' he held up the two spools of tape 'and since we have kept close tabs on you and your business activities' he indicated to the files on his desk 'that makes very interesting reading indeed.' Anthony's mouth felt dry.

'You have the penchant for making enemies wherever you go Anthony as your actions have caused the demise of many either associated with you personally or in your business dealings. Even your employees find you obnoxious especially those you discarded without fair reason or just cause. So the dossier of your misdemeanors and actions, many bordering on or plainly illegal, making your current position indefensible if it should ever come to a court of law hearing.' Anthony's resentment of these two conniving bastards flared. How dare they think they can control him. His mind looked for a defence but nothing came. He needed to focus but it was hard, as he knew he was being backed into a corner that he may never come out of.

'What you are going to do Anthony is to gift your seventy five percent of Harvey Engineering back to Harvey Montague. You will also return the original of the agreement you stole with an undertaking that you have not kept any copies whatsoever in any format.' Hugh placed the stock transfer forms in front of Anthony and a pen for him to sign. Anthony picked up the forms and read them through. He knew he had been out maneuvered, as the evidence they had against him was compelling and if he took them down then he would fall to a greater depth from which he would be unable to extricate himself. Well done, Anthony chuckled to himself, picked up the pen and signed the stock transfer forms. He then signed the undertaking that he would not keep copies of the agreement. Harvey was to accompany him to pick up the original and any copies he had. Oh how the mighty have fallen he thought.

'Now, in regard to your petition to divorce Sophie, the following will apply.' Hugh's on a roll thought Anthony.

'Sophie is to receive Westwood House, the Bentley and an allowance of £150,000 per annum with an annual increase based on the CPI. Plus twenty percent, tax paid, of the sale of any assets currently held by you and any assets in which you have an equity stake either directly or indirectly.'

Anthony slowly read the document with all its qualifications, caveats, terms and conditions that tied him legally into something he didn't want nor planned. Fuck Sophie, Hugh and Harvey, fuck everyone, even the system that they used to screw him out of what he had worked so hard to build into a substantial portfolio of wealth. It was beyond his comprehension to conceive let alone admit that most of what he had had been obtained by ruthlessly and relentlessly screwing anyone and everyone who got in his way or even if they didn't. He unconsciously gained much sadistic pleasure in denigrating and destroying their very existence. The injustice he felt was overwhelming. How could they do this to him? After all he had kept his word not to disclose their plot to defraud the system and in turn they had played him to checkmate. Anthony decided that he had to break all connection with Sophie, Hugh and Harvey and his past and make a fresh start.

'I agree to the terms of the divorce settlement except for the per annum payment of one hundred and fifty thousand and twenty percent of proceeds on the sale of my assets to Sophie. Instead, I will gift the residual twenty five percent holding in Maddison & Chapman to Sophie in lieu of.'

Hugh and Harvey glanced at each other. Hugh reached into his brief case and handed another stock transfer form to Anthony.

'No, I will buy your Maddison & Chapman twenty five percent holding for five hundred thousand.' Hugh placed the buyout offer in front of Anthony. Again Anthony realised he had been manipulated into a position he didn't fully comprehend the implications of. He needed time.

'The one hundred and fifty thousand stands."

'I'll think about it.' Anthony replied lamely.

'Nothing to think about Anthony, you will do as I say, sign.' Hugh's tone was dark and menacing.

Anthony picked up the pen and signed the documents. Once Hugh had all the documents he read through them and then reached into his briefcase to retrieve a personal cheque made out to Anthony Drax for £500,000. Anthony was amazed that all had been pre-planned; they knew exactly what the outcome would be.

Harvey followed Anthony to Peterborough to collect the original agreement he had stolen and the two other copies Anthony had made. Anthony opened the door of his apartment for Harvey.

'Before I go Anthony I need to inform you that an interim general manager with several security people are at Harvey Engineering this very minute. You will not be allowed entry and your personal effects from the office will be delivered here tomorrow morning at nine a.m. Next Monday representatives from an American multinational engineering company are coming to take over as I have sold Harvey Engineering for ten million pounds, that in my calculation will yield two and a half million pounds for Sophie's twenty five percent stake.' The colour drained from Anthony's face. Harvey turned and walked down the front steps. Half way down he stopped and turned to face the ashen-faced Anthony who looked very dejected at that moment.

'By the way, Hugh has sold Maddison & Chapman who will retain the Harvey Engineering account at the inflated fee for service you charged, a critical piece of the sale. All's well that ends well don't you think Anthony.' Harvey had a spring in his step as he walked towards his car. The night was warmer than usual and the air fresh. There was no sign of Anthony as he drove away.

❖

Anthony sat at his usual bar stool in the White Swan staring into his Farcet Mill Ale. Those bastards he had screwed in the first place had screwed him over but with a greater of sophistication. Even so he was pleased that all ties were severed and his past with a stroke of a pen was gone forever. He had taken stock of what he had, the apartment, car and £1.2 million plus the £1.8 million in his offshore account that had evaded detection and of course Julie, the very reason he was in this situation but on the other hand it probably would have happened sometime. He had lost an impressive fortune. Strangely, it felt good to be away from Teddington, the Matthews family and London overall leaving him free for his life in Peterborough, a relationship with Julie.

Simon was doing well at Harvey Engineering although the Americans had come in like a tornado sweeping everything clean before it, leaving new management and systems in its wake with further changes to be made. Simon had been promoted temporarily and ear marked as an integral part of the team. He was young, qualified and proven so would fit nicely with the new aggressive goal orientated, bottom line high profits strategy of the new managers with their American business psyche. No Mr nice guys doing favours or dead wood held for compassionate reasons. Twenty percent of clients had been axed within the first three days with shockwaves reverberating throughout the region. There were thirty-four staff in redundancy discussions with Human Resources so it was all happening at Harvey Engineering. The irony was no one suspected that Anthony hadn't received a bean from the sale so he was seen as a predatory multi millionaire by all and sundry as his enemy list grew. Anthony decided that he would reinvent himself quickly as he needed not only the challenge but to keep up appearances and propagate the ruse of being a multi-millionaire. To this end he ordered an Aston Martin to be delivered as soon as possible. His reinvention would be at the expense of other people and their money of course, a strategy he had used so successfully in the past. This had been and would remain his business strategy irrespective of the consequences it had for others as long as he made money on their backs.

The White Swan was a traditional English pub, tired, superficially clean with the odour of stale beer forever present, yet it had the warmth of dark oak beams and wood work and a retained small section of sixteenth century stonework near the entrance as a reminder of the coach inn that had originally stood on this site. The original inglenook had been rediscovered during renovations and remained a central feature. During the winter it kept the pub warm and cosy for the local patrons who were drawn to the pub as their fathers and grandfathers had been before. Anthony watched Toby Thornton draw pints for the four-burley farmers who had just come in and were focussed on intense conversation that augmented the murmur throughout.

'Same again Anthony?' Anthony hadn't noticed that Toby had approached.

'Thanks.' Toby took his empty and pulled the pint in a clean glass.

'You're a bit quiet tonight, thought you would be celebrating with your recent win.' Toby placed the Farcet Mill in front of Anthony.

'Bit of an anti-climax actually now that its over I'm afraid I need to look for new opportunities.' He took a swig of beer enjoying the taste of the golden ale.

'Whatever happened to Ortan Brewery, Toby?'

'Still there, although not for much longer I suspect, as it has made a loss every year for the past five years so I suspect Fortescue is going to cut his losses. It's a basket case, probably only worth scrap value as its only real asset is Farcet Mill Ale.' Toby moved away to serve other customers waiting patiently at the bar. Anthony was toying with the idea that there may be an opportunity here when he felt a light tap on his shoulder and turned.

'Hi you.' Julie smiled warmly and kissed him on the cheek as much for those who may have been watching as for Anthony. 'Thought we may go to the Hyde for dinner, what do you think?' Anthony put his arm around her waist and drew her close.

'Do you mind if we stay here? I could settle for an ale pie if that's alright?'

'Well you really know how to impress a girl!' Julie laughed. 'No, that's fine my darling, ale pie it is. There's a spare table over by the window. A G&T for me please.' She kissed his cheek again and walked towards the table while Anthony looked longingly at her delicious shape before beckoning Toby.

The ale pie was edible but lacked the richness of taste so often found with pub food. They decided to go back to Anthony's apartment where Julie spent much of her time these days as they had settled into a comfortable routine that was refreshing for Anthony. Julie never inquired about his work as such and yet supported him in all other aspects of his life. Her strong personality somehow worked with him purely because most things she said or did he was in agreement with.

It was on the following Monday that Anthony went to see his personal lawyer, Sandy Milford all of six foot six inches, thin of face and body with his silver steel rimmed glasses perched on the end of his large nose. Anthony never ceased to be amazed at the size of his large hands as they shook in greeting, a grip that always seemed on the cusp of crushing every bone in Anthony's hand but surprisingly didn't. Anthony wondered why he was called Sandy, as his hair was jet black as well as being a little greasy surely it wasn't his birth name.

'Anthony, good to see you, what can I do for you?' Always to the point thought Anthony, Sandy never entered into small talk.

'I hear that the Ortan Brewery may come up for sale and I am interested in purchasing it if I can get it for the right price. Have you heard anything about the brewery Sandy?'

'Just rumours that are much along the lines of what you said, nothing definite.'

'I know the brewery has made losses over the past few years and that Fortescue is considering a fire sale to cut his own losses. The indication is apart from the Farcet Mill Ale it has nothing to offer. The assets of the brewery are old technology with maintenance a high cost item so apart from turning sales around it is going to take a lot of capital to bring it up-to-date. I would like to commission you, Sandy, to carry out a feasibility study into its viability and asset value including land as soon as possible without anyone being aware. Furthermore it would be helpful if you could find out what Fortescue is planning and I'll see what information I can get for you to help.'

Sandy took an engagement agreement out of a folder from the top left hand side draw of his impressive oak desk then unscrewed the top off his Mont Blanc Scipione Borghese fountain pen to fill out the relevant sections of the engagement. Anthony knew the pen was expensive and guessed it had probably cost in the vicinity of seven thousand pounds, very much more than his standard Mont Blanc and made a mental note to rectify the discrepancy. However, the fact that Sandy's Omega Speedmaster watch was no match for his Hublot Classic Fusion worth five times the Omega gave some satisfaction as his wry smile indicated. Anyway his Aston Martin would be here tomorrow with two hundred and fifty miles on the clock was technically a demo model but no one would know and it has been useful to screw the London dealer down on the price and the private lease deal had been very favourable in conserving his capital.

'When do you want the report completed Anthony?'

'By next Friday.'

'For God's sake man, that's a big ask in four days? Not doable I'm afraid.'

'It is doable Sandy. I'm not paying your exorbitant fees to have this drag out. There are plenty of accountants out there who can do it for a mere pittance without loading up their fees. At the very least the valuation is the critical part of this and there is enough information on public record to get started. I'll have further information to you tomorrow. Make sure you get whoever does the work to sign a non disclosure agreement.'

Anthony signed the engagement agreement.

Sandy chuckled. 'Always a pleasure doing business with you Anthony, now let me get on with my real paying work.'

They arose shook hands and Anthony left.

As soon as he was outside he took out his mobile phone and called the White Swan.

'Toby, its Anthony, how are you?'

'Fine Anthony and you.'

'Are you available for lunch at the Hyde say one pm?'

'Unusual for a Monday, actually unusual for any day for me as I have only been to the Hyde Club once and that was a charity function.' Anthony waited patiently as he wasn't interested in anything Toby did or felt. 'What's it about?'

'I'll tell you when we are there Toby. See you at the Hyde.'

Toby had showered and dressed in suit and tie for the occasion. As Toby walked into the Hyde Club, Anthony sat in the foyer watching him go to reception and thought it is unfortunate for a person like Toby that no matter what he did or wore he always looked dishevelled, even in a tuxedo Anthony guessed he would look scruffy. Anthony walked to reception.

'I have a table booked in the restaurant Toby.' Toby spun around.

'Didn't see you there Anthony, sorry.'

'Not to bother, come on lets go in.' They walked into the restaurant that was about a quarter full with a few business men but mostly groups of well dressed women who probably frequented the place every lunch time given the well padded shapes on suffering seats.

'Good afternoon Mr Drax, this way please.' The waiter showed them to Anthony's regular window table he used for business lunches.

'Drinks gentlemen.'

'Toby.'

'Is it alright if I order a bottle of red wine?' Toby looked at Anthony.

'Anything you want Toby, you are my guest.'

'A bottle of house red please.' Anthony smiled at the lack of sophistication Toby showed, surely he should have a dozen wines he could recount but then again pubs are about beer and not often wine.

'The usual.' The waiter nodded to Anthony and floated off to get a bottle of house red and a TG&T.

They entered into small talk and reviewing the menu while waiting for their drinks. Drinks arrived and orders taken Anthony looked directly at Toby.

'The reason I invited you to lunch is for some privacy so I could discuss the feasibility of me purchasing the Ortan Brewery.'

Toby looked startled.

'I am not one hundred percent sure its up for sale Anthony it's just hearsay and the grumblings of Fortescue at board meetings really. Nothing definite at this stage.'

'But you would think that an acceptable offer for the brewery would be welcomed by Fortescue wouldn't you Toby?'

'Probably but are you serious? It doesn't make economic sense as the board has made countless efforts to see how it could be turned around and without a substantial capital injection its not going to work.' Toby was struggling to see a way forward. 'Although with the sale of Harvey Engineering I suppose it could be possible.' Anthony didn't correct Toby's misconception.

'I am very serious about this Toby and need you to help me do the deal. Of course I will make it worth your while.' Toby fell for it, immediately seeing the pound signs.

'How can I help you?'

Their lunch was served with Toby's filet mignon and a double serving of chips distracting him from the conversation while he poured his third glass of wine.

'If you are able to help me do a deal I will give you a purchase option for fifteen percent of the equity that with your existing five percent will give you a twenty percent holding in the company.' More pound signs flashed before Toby, as Anthony knew they would. Offer the carrot before the demand.

'How about we eat our lunch and you tell me everything you know about the business and its assets then we can decide on what we need to get this completed.'

Toby finished his bottle of red wine with his meal and his loose tongue had given a very thorough overview, warts and all. He told about the poor management of the board who were more interested in the food and beer at each meeting than the business. Fortescue had briefings, agenda and minutes typed out for each meeting so there were no decisions as the Board's purpose was to rubber stamped what Fortescue wanted. Fortescue was not a good businessman and his decisions were more often than not detrimental for the company adding to the demise of Ortan Brewery. The staff were not incentivised or accountable therefore complacent about productivity, quality and profit, as long as they were paid who cares. Toby had a large desert wine with his double serving of sticky toffee pudding while he dredged up everything about the business and Fortescue. He knew where all the bodies had been buried and who had buried them including many on the council. Anthony listened attentively to the incestuous web that had been weaved over time and was sure he was getting more than Toby would have given if he had been sober.

'How about we go to the bar and have a cleansing ale Toby? One for the road don't you think?'

'Definitely, sounds like a plan.'

They sat at the bar over a pint of ale, the first alcoholic drink for Anthony, Toby was far in excess of the official limit as he was a heavy drinker but unlike Anthony he didn't hold it well.

'What documents do you have concerning the brewery Toby?'

'I have a lever arch file holding all the documents issued at board meetings for each year, five files in all. I think they are in the cellar at the white Swan. Other than that nothing else.'

'Can I have a look at the files?'

'I'll get them out as soon as possible.' Toby slurred.

'Look Toby, you have too much to drink to drive, so I'll drive you back to the White Swan and pick up the files.'

Anthony walked into Sandy Milford's office carrying the five files he had retrieved from Toby and placed them on the side table.

'Here's something that'll keep your people busy Sandy.'

'I'll have them couriered to them now and by the way your report will be ready at the end of play Friday. Always the impossible for you Anthony.'

'I don't expect anything less Sandy. By the way, can you give me a quote for you to handle the legals on the purchase of the Ortan Brewery? Include your fee from this lot. I'll pay you the consulting fee as long as its open book.'

'No one else would pull a stunt like this. You're incorrigible Anthony and always have been.'

'Much more to come Sandy.'

Sandy watched Anthony drive past his office window wondering what was to come if anything, but then he had sold Harvey Engineering for a rumoured ten million so he had better keep onside. To date Anthony had probably cost him more than he made out of him or at least he was a break even, the wily sod.

Anthony took delivery of the Aston Marton the following morning and drove to the White Swan where Toby was out front talking to a delivery driver. He saw Toby watch the car for some time and he was surprised when it pulled up and Anthony got out. The delivery driver drove away as Toby walked over to the car.

'So is it true you made a packet from the sale of Harvey Engineering then.' He walked slowly around the car admiring its sleek lines. It's an icon of luxury and prestige of which Anthony was well aware and had purchased it for that very reason.

'Do you mind if I sit in it?'

'Not at all, go for it, a sign of things to come for you Toby.'

'I hope so.'

'Have you thought of anything else Toby?'

'Not really.' Toby was preoccupied with the luxurious interior as he sat low to the ground realising that if not this car then something else such as a Land Rover, more his style.

'Well if you do, give me a call.'

Anthony called Julie and talked her into taking the rest of the afternoon off with the threat of a refreshing drink at the Hyde before going back to his apartment for a light dinner and relaxing for the evening. He walked into her office to see her on the phone and she waved him into the settee while she finished.

'All done.' She said as she picked up her bag following him out.

'Is this yours?' The Aston Martin glistened in the afternoon sun.

'Yes.'

'Oh my God its amazing, when did you get it?'

'This afternoon.'

'Why didn't you tell me Anthony?'

'I didn't tell anyone. Come on let's go.'

Julie sat back in the plush leather passenger seat enjoying the luxury of the Aston Martin. Little was said until they arrived at the Hyde Club. If this is a sign of things to come then she had snagged the right guy.

'I'm impressed Anthony. Such a lovely car, what next I wonder?'

'Drinks at the bar for starters, come on.'

They walked hand in hand to the bar and settled for a G&T and a TG&T.

'I'm driving.' Anthony said as he raised his glass.

'Cheers. Here's to our future.'

'Cheers my dear, to our future.'

Anthony reached into his pocket and withdrew a small plain matt black box.

'A present for you.'

She opened it to see a diamond encrusted 24 carat gold ring of perfect design.

'Its breathtakingly beautiful Anthony but how did you know this is the design I like.'

'I do take notice when we are out shopping.' He smiled.

She slipped it onto her ring finger, a perfect fit. She raised her eyebrows.

'Now, what's the occasion? New car, new ring but how did you know finger size?'

'I checked your jewellery box. Very simple really.' He looked nonplussed. 'Every girl needs an engagement ring and every child need a father. Time to set the date for a quiet discrete wedding don't you think?'

Anthony collected the report with supporting documentation from Sandy on Friday afternoon for digestion over the weekend. By Sunday afternoon he was ready to meet with Samuel Hetherington. Julie had an event over the weekend for which Anthony was thankful as although she was a not in your face girl her very presence was sometimes unsettling for him. At least he was able to concentrate.

'I need you to arrange a meeting with Samuel Hetherington for tomorrow afternoon at two pm at the Hyde Club.' Anthony had arranged breakfast with Toby at the local early morning café where he knew Toby would order a full English with double serving of bacon, a heart attack on a plate. Toby's culinary habits left much to be desired and were reflected in his pale bloated body with skin blemishes. Anthony opted for porridge and honey with an orange juice that turned out to be a sugary substitute that annoyed him. He sent the orange juice back for a replacement black coffee. The crass plastic table covering was overshadowed by Toby's gluttony but Anthony reminded himself he still needed to lose weight and he needed Toby.

'Short notice Anthony. He may not be available.' Much to Anthony's disgust Toby was talking with his mouth half full spitting flecks of food over the table.

'Listen Toby, I don't care how you do it but tomorrow at two or it's off. So just do it'

'I'll do my best.' Toby was subdued.

'Make sure you're both on time. Catch you tomorrow.' Anthony sucked in the fresh air as he walked towards the Aston Marton. The café was oppressive and smelt of years of stale grease and unwashed bodies, he felt slightly nauseous. Back in his apartment he went through the documents again and the strategy to use in his negotiations. He showered, dressed casually for a relaxing afternoon, poured a red wine and had just sat down in the leather lounge chair when his mobile rang.

'I need to have something in writing on the options if I am going to assist you with this deal Anthony' said Toby with a touch of pleading that reflected his desperation.

'When the deal is done you'll get your options and not before.' Anthony was terse and direct. 'Have you spoken to Samuel?'

'Yes. He will be there at two. Demanded to know what it was about so I told him it was concerning an interest in the brewery. I think he took it as an investment rather than a purchase. I didn't give anything else so he seemed satisfied and agreed.'

'Good. I'll see you at two.' He hung up.

The first glass of wine went to his head, which was rare. Must be something to do with too much concentrating over the past few days. He needed something to eat so ordered a peperoni pizza to be delivered. Julie called to say she was shattered after a hectic weekend and was going to get an early night. They chattered until the pizza arrived. Pizza is the last thing I need to lose weight but I love pizza Anthony thought. He opened the box and poured another glass of wine

Anthony watched as Toby and Samuel came into the Hyde Club chatting as they looked around. Why do farmers wear tweed for a business meeting? Like a uniform, he thought, as is a pinstriped suit to the legal profession. He arose just as they spotted him. After greetings he led them into bar area where a secluded booth had been reserved. Drinks ordered Anthony decided to get down to business as he loathed inane small talk.

'I want to buy the Ortan Brewery and offer five hundred thousand, a first and final offer, lock, stock and all barrels except for any debt of course.'

Samuel and Toby looked startled. Toby took a long draft from his pint and remained silent. Samuel sized Anthony up with a steely look of distrust.

'Make it one point five million and we have a starting point' Samuel said quietly 'there are thirty acres of land worth at least one million, three hundred thousand for the brewery itself which is a going concern bringing in a revenue stream let alone the goodwill. Five hundred thousand is insulting.' Samuels face glowed red more with humiliation than anger.

'Thirty percent of the land has deteriorating buildings covering it that will cost a minimum of seven hundred and fifty thousand to bring them up to basic standard with another thirty percent covered in tarmac or gravel that needs urgent repair. The rest of the land has an Environmental Authority order to deal with the years of pollution that according to the quotes you already have will cost over nine hundred thousand. As far as a going concern, over the past five years the business has operated at increasing losses so the company is in debt to five hundred thousand that has to be settled within ninety days. Furthermore Samuel, the goodwill is negative as the whole thing is a car crash waiting to happen. My offer stands for the next hour, after that I walk away.' Anthony placed the report and a sale agreement in front of a stunned Samuel Hetherington. Samuel was amazed at the detail in the report showing many negative aspects of the business even he wasn't aware of. How in the hell did it get to such a disastrous state? The family had been hounding him to either sell it or get an investment partner to salvage something before it goes into administration. The stress was overwhelming.

'This isn't going to happen Anthony as the land and scrap value is more than one and a half million for God's sake. We need to protect the jobs of the employees as some have been there for over twenty-five years. The area needs this business and we have a responsibility to everyone in the area.' Samuel was struggling though deep down he knew it was the end. It would be a relief to be rid of the whole damn thing and five hundred thousand would come in handy. Let the bank fight Anthony for the debt. That will show the arrogant bastard I'm not to be dictated to.

'You have fifty minutes to make your decision.' Anthony knew the Hetherington family had nowhere else to go.

'I will need to get approval from the family on this Anthony as the shares are held in trust. It will take time. I can get back to you by the end of the week.'

'You have absolute power of attorney over the family trust on this matter so all it needs is your signature on the deed of sale. You now have forty minutes then I walk.' Anthony had all the aces.

How did Anthony know about the trust, it was not in the public domain. Samuel realised that the only disclosure had been in a board minute relating to the loan he had taken out from the employee's pension pot some years ago. There was no way Anthony had access to the minutes. If he doesn't take this deal Samuel knew he would be lumbered with the whole mess to sort out. He was sick and tired of the bloody brewery and didn't think he had the energy or will to carry on let alone resolve the mess. He had to take the deal. Without a further word Samuel took out his pen, signed and dated the bill of sale and his resignation from the board of directors. Anthony passed the document to Toby who hadn't uttered a word during the exchange.

'I need you to witness this Toby.' Toby did as he was instructed.

The stock transfer form was also signed giving Anthony a ninety five percent holding with Toby having the other five percent. Anthony had total control.

'What about the £500,000 payment.' Samuel blurted out.

'I have a cheque for £500,000 made out to the company bankers which I will deposit this afternoon and that will clear the company's debt.'

Samuel looked totally dejected, beaten as Anthony arose from the table and said he needed to be somewhere else.

'Toby, I need to see you at five so I will come down to the White Swan.' He left them sitting looking out of the large window facing into the beautiful English garden that was suddenly lit by a shaft of sunlight breaking through the ominous dark cloud canopy that had covered the region for the past three days. Samuel smiled to himself. At least I can walk away with peace of mind and free from this millstone around my neck. Free at last. Samuel walked with Toby past the reception to the relief of a fresh start.

'Mr Hetherington' the receptionist waved to Samuel 'Mr Drax said you would settle the bill.' Samuel laughed out loud.

'Of course, pleased to do that.' He paid the drinks bill. 'The least I can do.' He smiled to himself. Toby had left.

'Mr Drax also left this envelope for you.'

Samuel sat in his car and opened the large envelope and withdrew the thirty-day call for the two hundred and fifty thousand personal loan that had been made some years before to Samuel Hetherington from the Ortan Brewery pension fund. Anthony had no intention of these funds going anywhere near the pension fund as it was destined for his pocket.

Toby was pulling a pint when Anthony walked into the bar at the White Swan.

'A pint of the usual.' Toby said

'Not at the moment as I need to attend to something else. I just wanted to get you to sign the option agreement we discussed.' Toby was transparently delighted.

'I'll look it over and get back to you.'

'You have five minutes read and sign it, I'm in a hurry.' Anthony passed two copies of the agreement to Toby.

'Jeez Anthony, your impossible.'

'If you don't want it I'll get going. The opportunities are great for someone who has nothing.' Toby felt the sting as he reluctantly started to read the agreement.

'There is so much in this, I should really get some legal advice.'

'It's a standard options agreement, just sign it Toby, I need to go.' Anthony passed his pen to Toby.

Toby hesitated and then signed both copies passing one back to Anthony who put it in his briefcase.

'There is a couple of other matters we need to discuss so I'll come down tomorrow evening for that pint.' Without anything further Anthony left.

❖

Julie was waiting for him when he got back to the apartment, wine poured and dinner simmering on the stove. He needed to get the wedding out of the way as there was much to do on the home and business fronts.

'I had confirmation that all is in order for our civil ceremony at the London Registry Office for Friday of next week. Simon has taken some time of work so will be there however Emma is not coming. Small but sweet darling.' Julie took a sip of her wine and busied herself with dinner.

'I'll have a beer first.' Anthony took a cold Theakston's Old Peculiar from the fridge and poured it into a Theakston glass, sipped and savoured the rich bitter taste.

'I think we should stay down in London after the wedding for a couple of days as a precursor to our honeymoon.'

'What honeymoon?' Julie teased.

'That's for you to sort out Miss events manager.' Anthony smiled. 'I also spoke to Simon today and he seemed quite chipper about our wedding so all good there' no mention of Emma 'By the way after we are married I'll get you to find a place for the three of us to live.'

'We have a place to live, here.' Julie looked quizzically at Anthony. What's he thinking? Early days Mr Drax she said to herself.

'No, I want something much bigger, an investment that gives us some luxury and status while providing room to keep your horses.'

'I don't have any horses.' Julie was confused.

'But you ride at least three time a week so its about time you had your own don't you think. You always wanted to breed horses so perfect opportunity to turn your hobby into a business.' He needed to keep her busy and out of his hair as business was going to get messy and very demanding but the rewards would be significant.

New house and horses, this guy works fast just as Julie liked it. She was as ambitious and but less selfish than Anthony which was the lynch pin of their relationship except he would bring in the money and she would help him spend it, all in the plan.

Buoyed by their mutual agreement on most things and the future they ate dinner, drank wine and talked details into the night. She ensured their night was sealed with strong sensual love making that while mutually satisfying she knew was critical to keeping Anthony comfortable and committed. The child would be another issue though his record as a father left much to be desired.

Signing the share option agreement bolstered Toby, although there were a couple of grey areas however he envisaged much more to come. This was his time, he had worked hard all his life with little to show for it and now he was an integral part of Anthony Drax's business plan and future to which he would make sure he would become indispensable. The Anthony's of this world would come and go but Toby Thornton would take his opportunity to ensure he would make his own fortune riding on their backs.

Anthony had picked up the documents from Sandy Milford before he met with Toby.

'Hi Toby, time to earn your options. Firstly, there are three other directors on the board other than you and myself. I have their resignations that you will get them to sign leaving the two of us as the only directors.'

'You haven't even met them yet.' Anthony gave Toby a penetrating steely look.

'Secondly, you will terminate the managing director and finance director plus these people on this list. The only people I want at this stage are those who are directly involved with the production of Farcet Mill Ale. You will tell the master brewer that he is to receive a fifty percent pay rise and an annual bonus of five thousand pounds to ensure production and supply to existing clients runs smoothly.' Toby was stunned not only at the severity of the actions Anthony had taken but also that he had to fire the bullets, do all the dirty work.

'How much is my remuneration for this?'

'An option agreement.' Anthony wasn't interested in remunerating anyone else but himself so set ten thousand per month and an expenses allowance into his private company.

Toby was distraught at having to be the hatchet man, after all he had grown up here and knew most of the people he had to chop, some of them were his friends. Doesn't this guy have any appreciation of his position or the effect it was going to have on the families?

'I will be back in a weeks when I expect you to have this completed as there is much more to do if we are going to pull Ortan Brewery out of the red into a going concern.'

Anthony left the White Swan and went straight around to Sandy's office to action the remaining steps to be taken. By the end of three days he had sold all of the assets from the brewery, including the rights to the brand name Farcet Mill Ale to his private company for one pound, set up another company into which the thirty acres of land was sold at the princely sum of one pound leaving Ortan Brewery without any assets or land but still holding all the staff and liabilities including the now empty pension fund that went with them. The production of Farcet Mill Ale, from now on, would be under licence from Anthony to Ortan Brewery Limited with all of the profits going directly to Anthony's company as the license fee. By the time Anthony had returned from his wedding all had been completed for the next stage in the demise of Ortan Brewery.

The wedding was surprisingly good fun with the ceremony carried out efficiently and painlessly in what surely had to be record time, much to the joy of the three of them who immediately after headed to the Crossed Keys pub around the corner to celebrate with a bottle of champagne that naturally led to two bottles before they headed back to the five star hotel where Julie had booked an executive suite for her and Anthony and a standard room for Simon. They dined at Langan's Brassiere without seeing any celebrities, which didn't bother them at all as the food was superb, champagne magnificent and ambiance what everyone expected. By the end of the evening the staff were pleased to see the inebriated noisy party of three, fall into a black cab and drive away. They staggered into the bar at the hotel for a nightcap, laughing and talking over each other. Within minutes Simon had fallen asleep while Anthony finished his beer and Julie her water. Anthony and Julie half carried Simon to his room, took off his shoes and coat before allowing him to fall unceremoniously onto his bed. They retired without comment to their room where they also fell into a deep slumber.

'Good morning, you two.' Simon had showered and dressed casually to join Mr and Mrs Drax for breakfast. Multiple cups of coffee with little to eat was the order of the day before Simon got up to get a cab to Kings Cross Station for his train back to Peterborough.

'Well Mr and Mrs Drax I'll be seeing you back home in the not too distant future I hope. Thanks for asking me to take part in your wedding as it was a great time and the only family function I have been to in years, although I will be feeling the effects for a few hours I suspect.'

'It was marvellous to have you with us and I'll call when back, safe trip dear and take care.' Julie gave Simon a warm hug in genuine appreciation for his acceptance of her into this relationship.'

'No problems wicked step mother, looking forward to many a free meal.' Simon smiled warmly and turned towards his father.

'Thanks son for coming down, we need to talk soon as something has come up that you may be interested in. Have a good trip.' They shook hands and Simon left.

Anthony and Julie retired to their room feeling very seedy. They slept it off before going back to the bar for an afternoon pre-dinner drink, hair of the dog, saviour of all as Anthony would say. The shower had refreshed them enough to consummate their new marital status before pre-dinner drinks, followed by more consummation in earnest the next day. Julie ensured Anthony was well rewarded and satisfied for the leap of faith he had taken with her. Anthony was satisfied that he had given Julie what every wife expected on her wedding weekend.

10

Peter Montgomery was as dodgy as a snake oil salesman. On his father's death he had inherited his father's very successful real estate business but unfortunately Peter didn't have the acumen or ethics of his father so the business steadily declined. He was desperate to pull it out of the slide and would do anything necessary if the opportunity arose. Peter was just the sort of person Anthony was looking for to complete the next stage of the Ortan Brewery plan.

'The way it stands now Peter is that I have thirty acres of prime real estate which I want you to arrange residential planning permission and then find a developer to buy the whole thirty acres.' Peter knew in his heart that this was the opportunity he had been waiting for, as the commission would be worth a fortune. He started to salivate.

'What commission can I expect?' Anthony knew he had the right person immediately as his research had shown that Peter was suffering financially which he had just confirmed.

'In its current state the land is worth between thirty to forty thousand pounds an acre but with housing planning approval it would be worth one million pounds an acre, only if there is a developer willing to take it on. So, your commission will be one percent, that is three hundred thousand pounds on completion.'

'Five percent is more appropriate in a deal this complex Anthony especially when I will be putting the whole thing together.' The greed is showing thought Anthony.

'Alright, to compensate you I will agree to two percent but that is the final offer that you will either accept or I find someone else.' Anthony knew he would accept.

'Two percent it is then.'   Peter had already decided to negotiate another two percent from the developer a highly illegal and unscrupulous game to play but nevertheless Peter felt he could pull a double dip off without anyone finding out.

'I have the contract here that you have an hour to read and sign. If you don't sign it within the hour, its off.' Anthony gave the agreement to Peter.

'What's this about me having to provide an up front amount of two hundred and fifty thousand pounds for expenses?' Peter was only half way through the agreement and couldn't believe he was being asked to provide such funds.

'If you read the next paragraph you will see on completion the funds will be reimbursed in full with a ten percent premium, an amazing return wouldn't you say.' There was no way Anthony was using his own money to finance Peter's commission. Anyhow the personal risk was too great and he needed to put Peter under pressure.

'Where am I going to get the money from?' Anthony knew that Peter's wife owned a house valued in excess of three hundred thousand that she an only child had inherited from her mother when she passed away three years ago. Her father had died seven years previously.

'I am sure you are a resourceful person Peter and have the ability and contacts to arrange the finance.'

'So if I don't raise the money within thirty days I have to pay an abort fee of ten percent of the amount, so you walk away with twenty five thousand.'

'You don't have to sign Peter. Just give it back and leave, your choice.' Peter knew that if he gave this opportunity up he would potentially lose six hundred thousand pounds. That was too much to lose so he had to go with it but there was so many unknowns. He supressed common sense and risk while he only considered the pay out, a reflection of his desperation. He had some work to do which would require a magic wand to get all the ducks in a row. Peter signed the contract as he thought what the hell.

Life with Julie settled down into a comfortable routine that gave neither of them any grief as they went about their respective daily lives. Julie's pregnancy was unremarkable, almost a side issue apart from the swelling that notified all, of her condition. No morning sickness, tiredness, soreness or anything really just a bit of discomfort almost as though it was alien to her body. She continued to work as well as search for a house so they could move out of Anthony's apartment that he would put up for an executive lease. Julie's flat already had a long-term rental successfully agreed. The four home options she showed Anthony were on or near Thorpe Road and all had been fully redeveloped into modern prestige housing but for Anthony they were not quite what he had in mind although Julie was impressed and excited at the prospect of living in any one of them.

'No I don't object to any of them, its just not what I had in mind. They are good clean, well developed adequate houses and that's the problem, they are adequate.'

'Oh come on Anthony, they are more than adequate, in a great area, close to all amenities including schools. What is there not to like about them?'

Anthony was looking through the discards when he came across one that spiked his interest. Now this is more like it.' He passed the brochure to Julie.

'You have to be kidding me. It's a dump; what are you thinking about, its in the sticks away from everything.'

'It has twenty-two acres of land with stables. Absolutely perfect.'

It wasn't only that it was called Farcet Hall after his favourite beer but it was the building itself jumping out at him. A symmetrical building in local stone with rusticated corner stones and square groups of rusticated chimney shafts that all met the type of building in his minds eye. The fourth floor of three dormers framed by a slate roof was perfect and from the image it looked structurally sound. The inside rooms had high ornate ceilings with cornices to match and what looked like the library had oak panelled walls. It wasn't derelict, just tired, dusty and untidy both inside and out, nothing that couldn't be rectified with a little elbow grease. Yes, it was just what he wanted and he would beat the price down from the asking price of five hundred thousand to more like three hundred and seventy five thousand, Anthony thought, given it had been on the market for well over a year.

'I had no idea you were thinking of something so grandiose, my God, its huge and a little scruffy, don't you think?' Julie was in two minds. So much work but if it was fully refurbished it would be magnificent and fit in well with her vision of a new life with all the trappings. Actually, it was on the fringe of the town so really not too difficult to access facilities as well as being in a quiet part of the old residential area with little traffic. Then there were the stables. She hadn't seen this coming but knew if she played her cards right Anthony would buy Farcet Hall, so the strategy was not to seem too enthusiastic.

'I'll get you to notify the agent that I am interested and get him to arrange a building survey immediately. This is what I want so lets move on this and I'll negotiate the price I am willing to pay.' Julie realised that she didn't need a strategy, as it seemed Anthony had made up his mind and was determined to buy Farcet Hall.

Much to his surprise, Peter Montgomery actually raised the two hundred and fifty thousand pound required by Anthony within two days of signing the contract. He had approached two of his father's very wealthy cronies who had both retired and were always dabbling in some investment or scheme to make more money. The loan was at great expense, as they required thirty five percent of his commission to be covered by a personal guarantee from Peter's wife against her house. So all up they would nearly double their investment. He knew his wife would not agree to the guarantee so he forged her signature and paid one of his associates to witness the signature. The guarantee was registered.

'I have the funds in my client account.' Peter said to Anthony over the phone.

'Have you a pen and paper?' Anthony didn't trust Peter one iota 'I'll give you the coordinates for my private company bank account and you will have the funds transferred by five this afternoon. I'll reimburse all acceptable costs in putting the deal together. Remember, don't commit to any expenditure without my approval.'

'No need for that as I'll look after the funds Anthony and give you monthly management accounts for the expenditure.' Peter had already withdrawn £10,000 to pay minimum payments to five creditors who had been hounding him for months. He started to sweat.

'Read your contract, then have the funds transferred Peter.' Anthony hung up. No way Peter would control the expenditure as if there were any funds left they were for him not Peter, the cheeky git.

The survey from Farcet Hall came back as expected, structurally sound but everything else needing attention. Not quite a basket case so it should be knocked into shape relatively easy. Anthony knew it was undervalued and he would drive the price down even further so the investment was attractive. He estimated to get it into shape and with the extension he was going to add he needed a budget of eight hundred thousand that included the purchase price, however the end value of the asset would be at least double.

'What did you think of the building survey?' Julie handed Anthony a glass of red wine as he sat at the breakfast bar to watch her to prepare dinner.

'As expected, no real problems and a very good investment overall.' Good for your ego thought Julie.

'So Farcet Hall is a good option then? But surely we should discuss the house options and see which is the best overall don't you think.' Julie was still in two minds as to what was the best choice and was teetering on one of the Thorpe Road properties close to everything especially schools and health centre for the baby. She laid a hand on her bulge feeling the slight response from within.

'Nothing to discuss, I purchased the Hall this afternoon. Knocked them down to four hundred thousand as a cash buyer so saved a hundred thousand not bad for an afternoons work.' Julie was not really shocked as this was the way Anthony worked, no consultation with her and if truth was known she was comfortable with it as half the asset was technically hers.

'I don't suppose the Hall will be ready in three months for the arrival of the baby.' She knew it wouldn't be.

'It will be habitable in six months and the extension will take twelve months to complete.'

'What extension?' This was news to Julie.

'I'm having a large orangery extension built on the back of the house for the indoor pool, sauna and gym plus a casual sitting area all under one roof.'

'Have you already arranged the plans and contracts?'

'No.'

'How are you so sure about the renovation and build times then?'

'A guestimation really but it will be a negotiated penalty contract that will protect me. Don't worry I'll make sure the penalties kick in so I can recoup some of the budget as better in my pocket than theirs.' Julie gave up. He was always looking to take advantage or screw someone or another. No wonder his reputation was mixed and if he continued it would get worse but she knew Anthony didn't care what other people thought. No reasons to rock the boat either as she was just an innocent party who would receive sympathy rather than the condemnation she knew would eventually come. Innocent party. Julie liked the sound of that especially now that she was indirectly accruing a tidy net worth that was topped with an enviable elite life style. This will do for the moment Mr Drax. Marriage does have its benefits.

Toby Thornton looked totally dejected as Anthony sat at the bar in the White Swan.

'Business not doing well?' Anthony knew it wasn't.

'You've put me in an unenviable position Anthony.'

'I hope you have completed the tasks we discussed.' Anthony couldn't give a toss as to what position Toby was in as long as he had fired all the bullets.

'Yes, the directors have gone and at least half the staff have been sacked with the rest focussing on the production of Farcet Mill Ale the only product left. There was all hell to pay Anthony and I was in the firing line with talk of suing the company for wrongful dismissal. The new accountant you put in charge of the finances is an arrogant sod as well. Where is all this headed?'

Now that the land and other assets had been transferred out of Ortan Brewery there was nothing left for anyone to sue so they could do what they like. In fact, as the two hundred and fifty thousand that had been borrowed by Samuel Hetherington from the pension fund had been redirected to Anthony's account there was only unsecured debt in Ortan Brewery Limited that would soon cease to exist.

'Well done Toby, I knew I could count on you. You must be pleased that your options and equity have good future prospects?' As Toby's options and equity were in Ortan Brewery Limited that would soon be non-existent, they will be worthless, much to the amusement of Anthony. He knew Toby wouldn't think to check Companies House as all the changes were in the public domain but that was his problem and something Anthony counted on.

'Actually I have something else I want you to do. What do you know about Thruways Brewery?'

Thruways Brewery was the only other brewery in Peterborough, much older than Ortan Brewery and better run although a bit tired and needed new blood to take it forward. It managed to keep its head above water only due to the shareholders not receiving any dividends over the past nine years. A situation that annoyed them greatly and rumour was that it's unofficially up for sale at the right price.

'I know one of the board members through the Rotary Club. Other than that nothing really except that I heard it might be up for sale but nothing concrete. Who knows?'

'Do some digging and find out if it is available and arrange for me to meet with your contact.' Anthony feigned disinterest.

'What's in it for me.' Toby perked up.

'Nothing if nothing eventuates. However if you broker a deal then I'll make it worth your while.' Anthony finished his pint of ale and left with the carrot dangling. Toby looked as Anthony walked out of the pub. Just as he was getting spooked over having to do Anthony's dirty work in Ortan Brewery another opportunity comes up. It could actually turn out quite well with these two opportunities. It may very well give him enough to retire on and get out of the White Swan that he loathed with a vengeance. Like all his type, Toby was so predictable that they left themselves open for use and abuse. Anthony enjoyed playing them for his own benefit. They deserved it. He needed to keep Toby full of hope but locked into the White Swan as long as he needed him. He would discard him without a second thought.

There was no way that Peter Montgomery had the ability or contacts to entice a property developer to take on the Ortan Brewery thirty acre site so he was forced to go back cap in hand to his two investors who had fronted the initial two hundred and fifty pounds paid to Anthony. They were not too pleased as they had been led to believe that the developer was in place. They soon realised that they were in a salvage position and demanded equal shares in any residual profit above the returns on their initial investment. Peter had that sinking feeling that comes with the realisation he had bitten off more than he could chew. His prospects for a substantial financial gain were rapidly fading. It was the two investors who called in a favour from a London based developer convincing him that this property development deal was a deal to be had. Anthony had already engaged consultants to complete the information memorandum including an environmental study that surprisingly gave the site a clean bill of health overturning the original environmental order. Parker &

Shannon of London were encouraged by the report so decided to proceed with discussions with the owner Anthony Drax. Peter and his two investors negotiated a confidential commission with Parker & Shannon that was in Peter's name to assure anonymity for the investors. The council, conditional to the deal going ahead, had given tentative planning approval.

'It's a simple purchase transaction really. I have thirty acres of land with planning approval for residential housing, a very rare and profitable project in a developing town that is attractive to people working in London as commuting is readily available. The valuation is twenty two million with Parker & Shannon paying one million pounds on signing of contract, fifty percent on completion of the demolition of the Ortan Brewery and the residual monthly over twelve months.'

The purchase price was finally agreed at eighteen million pounds. Richard Parker had the legal agreements drawn up with both parties agreeing that all was in order including the standard disclosures that accompanied such agreements. Neither Peter Montgomery nor his investors were party to the agreements or discussions so had no realisation that their commission agreements had been fully disclosed in the transaction. Unfortunately for Peter both commission agreements had a no 'double dipping' clause in the fine print that not only precluded claiming commission from both Anthony Drax and Parker & Shannon but if he did then it would render the agreements null and void with the aggrieved parties able to claim damages.

Anthony and Richard Parker signed the agreements duly witnessed with the one million pounds to be deposited the following day into Anthony's account.

The initial renovations on Farcet Hall were completed one month after Karen Drax was born. Anthony attending a meeting in London didn't arrive at the hospital until four hours after the birth to find mother and child in their private bed. He had been annoyed at having to miss the evening dinner scheduled with senior management from Ranger Inc. who were looking to have their well established USA Passmore Beer produced under license in the United Kingdom. Anthony was on the shortlist for one of the licences.

'Sorry I wasn't here Julie. You look exhausted.'

'I am, after a three hour struggle to get this one out but she's gorgeous.'

Anthony looked at the large face framed by a blanket tightly wrapped around the somewhat disproportionate small body. He had no thoughts or emotions concerning this baby.

'Yes, obviously nothing wrong, all normal, ten fingers and toes as they say.'

Julie smiled to see Anthony struggle but she expected nothing less and knew Karen would be all hers until she was into her late teens when just maybe Anthony would become interested.

'How is business.' Julie said knowing this would get him talking.

'The London meeting went well and the sale of the Ortan Brewery site has gone through. The demolition of the brewery is scheduled to start in three months with the scrap value of just under two hundred thousand pounds being deposited into our company account at the end of next month. I am hopeful that I can buy Thruways Brewery, however nothing finalised yet which is annoying as the Passmore Beer production license depends on having this in place. I'm sure all will fall into place soon.' Anthony is so animated when talking about his business and how much has made from his wheeling and dealings thought Julie.

'Are you pleased with the renovations.' Julie couldn't wait to move into Farcet Hall, as having Karen in the apartment will be cramped and no doubt depressing.

'Unfortunately all is on time and budget so not likely to activate the penalty clause. Good to see the extension has started so another eight months and all should be finished. At least the extension won't interfere with living in the Hall.'

'When are you coming back to the apartment.' Anthony's peace and quiet would be shattered and he knew it. More time at the office needed he thought.

'Tomorrow. Can you pick us up?'

'Of course, I'll go now as need some sleep so give me a call tomorrow when you're ready.' He kissed her gently on the forehead, took a last look at Karen and left.

He had leased Julie a Range Rover through their company but kept the Aston Martin for himself although he was bored with it, as it had done its job in portraying an image he had needed to cultivate. Farcet Hall would bolster his business and social image in the minds of many within the community helping to convince all that he is a man of means and standing, not to be challenged or toyed with.

Many within the flotsam and jetsam of his past business savagery loathed Anthony for causing their demise to feather his own nest, a fact he supressed and distanced himself from while he migrated to the upper echelons of society and business but even there he was viewed with scepticism and caution. It was only the minions within the government agencies and academia that looked up to and envied Anthony.

He picked Julie and Karen up in her Range Rover from the hospital and took them back to the apartment.

❖

Four directors controlled over fifty percent of Thruways Brewery, built of red brick surrounding a steel frame from the nineteenth century, on the high street. Now supporting rusted corrugated storage additions adding to the run down look that annoyed councillors and residents alike. Jonathan Seymour, a spider naevi nosed, tweed clad retired farmer with an abrasive manner was, by default, the spokes person for the group. He didn't need the money but wanted rid of the brewery that threatened the remnants of a spurious reputation for being an astute businessman.

'Drax by name and brewer by occupation.' bellowed Seymour as he chuckled at his own poorly executed joke. The others sat in silence. A ripe one here thought Anthony. Toby Thornton smiled in support.

'So what do you have in mind or is it an offer?' Said Seymour as the question was direct and to the point which pleased Anthony. No small talk just cut to the chase.

'Five million, walk in walk out. First and final offer.' Anthony wasn't going to haggle even though it was three

million under the three valuations he had commissioned.
'One million down then one million a year for four years.'
This would give each of the four shareholders sitting around the table one million each and the other million shared between the residual shareholders.
'Now listen here Drax, the assets and business are worth at least ten million so we do need to negotiate I'm afraid.' Before he could continue Anthony got to his feet.
'I assume that's a no then gentlemen. Thank you for your time and all the best for the future.' Much to the dismay of all at the table he turned and started walking towards the door.
'Don't be so aggressive Drax. Come back and lets talk about this.'
'Nothing to talk about, you have my offer, its either a yes or no.' Anthony waited.
'At least give us time to discuss and consider your offer.' Seymour was flustered with his nose turning a deeper red than usual. He was used to getting his own way but had met more than his match.
'I'll be back in thirty minutes for your answer.' Anthony walked out of the room and went to the bar for a refreshing pint. He had called their bluff.
Exactly thirty minutes later he sat down at the table.
'Well?'
'We accept your offer on your terms.' Mumbled Jonathan Seymour with his cohorts nodding in agreement.
Anthony opened his briefcase and withdrew three copies of the sale contract that committed to the payment of the first one million in sixty days from the signing of the agreement. The four directors were surprised that all their

names were on the signature page. How did Anthony know they were coming as at least one of them only decided to attend the meeting at the last minute but then again none of them trusted Seymour. Anthony had sixty days to get Ranger Inc. on board, however, they had agreed in principle so it should be able to be finalised within time. Many a slip between cup and lip Anthony reminded himself. The key is to go in confident and assertive. Ranger Inc. would have done their due diligence and found that his private company had in excess of one million pounds cash and a positive trading record. He had substantial assets including Ortan Brewery and Farcet Hall. What was hidden was how he came about those assets and the pain and devastation he had caused many along the way. That was incidental to Anthony as winning was everything to ensure those who mattered gave him his due recognition although few did. Status was everything, he needed to be seen as successful and was driven to it. Anthony gained a perverse pleasure in causing others to suffer, a symptom of his long-standing psychotic narcissism that was his destiny and pleasure.

'What's my commission for pulling the deal in?' It was three days later when Anthony was sitting at the bar in the White Swan with an early afternoon Farcet Mill ale that Toby Thornton confronted him. He took a cheque from the inside pocket of his coat.

'I have one hundred thousand pounds here Toby.' Toby started to salivate as he reached out for the cheque.

'Not so fast my friend. There is something I want from you first.'

'But I have fulfilled my obligation. I brokered the deal as requested and more.' Toby was annoyed and suspected this was another of Anthony's shifty deals he had seen pulled on others so often. How he had come to loath this bastard.

'All you did was arrange a meeting and I brokered the deal. In recompense I have a cheque so do you want it or not?'

'Of course I do. It will be the first time you have paid for anything I have done for you.' Anthony made a mental note to punish Toby for his insubordination, a blatant disrespect. There would be future opportunities to plunge the dagger in.

'That's a bit harsh Toby after all you have your options. Now, for the one hundred thousand pounds you are going to sell me fifty percent of the White Swan.' Anthony pulled the sale agreements out of his briefcase and passed them to Toby. Toby signed all three and had them witnessed before handing two copies back to Anthony. One day, thought Toby, just one day I hope you get what's coming to you. Toby had sold Anthony his fifty percent share holding in the White Swan, his wife owned the other fifty percent. At least he could pay off his credit cards and several loans that had been outstanding forever and have some left over. The relief was palpable. After all he had his equity and options in Ortan Brewery. Anthony toyed with the idea of working on Toby's wife who was a slim, attractive somewhat reserved woman with a tell tale sparkle in her eyes that reflected a frustration with her overweight and distant husband whom she had fallen out of love, long ago and their relationship had waned into a non sexual unfeeling convenience.

It had been nine months since Anthony, Julie and Karen had moved into Farcet Hall and rented out the apartment. In total Anthony had spent nine hundred and eighty thousand pounds that included the renovations, extension, stables and landscaping completed on time and within budget which annoyed Anthony no end as he was hoping to be able to activate the penalty clause to claw back some of the expenditure. He did manage to withhold final payments until he received threats of legal action. He desperately needed to cause some disruption, cause some pain to those who had performed their work flawlessly, even though there was no logical or rational reason. Julie held her concern of such action as she knew it to be futile and she needed to maintain her lifestyle and that of her children. After all, Anthony had always been a means to her end. Four staff were recruited, two housemaids, a gardener and stable hand. All staff being employed through Ortan Brewery and would be transferred to Thruways Brewery in due course. Julie bought five horses and a horse float. The Aston Martin was traded in for another Range Rover and life settled into a pleasant routine for Julie and Anthony.

'We've come along way.' Julie was sat in the outdoor setting with Anthony.

He looked at her and thought, I've come along way and you've contributed nothing. He didn't worry too much as the freehold house was in his name and now valued at two million two hundred thousand. He had more than doubled his **investment**.

'Another champagne.' Julie passed him her flute. The Billecart-Salmon Blanc de Blancs was their regulars drink although with a free supply of Farcet Mill ale Anthony tended to over indulge most evenings and was often out of control on weekends. His drinking was of concern to Julie as he was an unpleasant drunk. She on the other hand was very conservative with her drinking as the family responsibilities fell on her. There was a stock of red and white wines with the special stash of Billecart-Salmon Brut Reserve nv Methuselah for special occasions where those who needed to be impressed, were.

'Actually I shouldn't be drinking at all.' Julie looked at Anthony and smiled. He immediately understood.

'This can't keep happening you know. We need to cap the children at two.'

'I am already three months. At least they will be close together and yes I agree, two children is the perfect number.' Two is two too many but Anthony kept his thoughts to himself. Their hot torrid sex days were well passed although Julie made sure supply met demand and initiated such events to nurture his ego and narcissistic needs. Anthony said nothing further about the pregnancy.

'Don't forget I already have two from my time with Sophie. Four is more than enough.'

'When was the last time you saw Emma?'

'Last Christmas, as she tends to focus on her mother as you know, although there doesn't seem to be any animosity which may be indifference on her part or both our parts.'

'She is always pleasant to me, I quite like her, perhaps you should make more of an effort.'

'I don't think she has forgiven me and probably never will but that's life. However I take your point but don't expect me to grovel and it wouldn't hurt her to make an effort after all I am her father.' Anthony was getting annoyed. Emma should show him some respect and recognise his successes. No doubt at some stage she will see the error of her ways.

'By the way, have you seen Simon recently?'

'Only last week we had coffee and a catch up. He's in fine form and doing well. Actually, I've been thinking of asking him to come into Thruways brewery as general manager.'

'Does he know anything about brewing?'

'Doesn't have to as the master brewer handles brewing, I only need him to handle the business side of things. Even though he lacks experience he will learn under my guidance, as I will be owner and chairman. Must have a talk to him.'

Julie had reservations about Anthony and Simon working together. Anthony poured himself another champagne; he's definitely happiest when he's drinking thought Julie.

Ranger Inc. had carried out its due diligence on the Thruways Brewery and Anthony with everything checking out. While the brewery had unused capacity to take on the initial production volumes required there was doubt about its ability to meet increasing volumes if required in the future. The most compelling aspect was location as it could service the national market entry in both the south and northern regions. Ranger's policy was market entry by stealth, keeping costs down and their head below the parapet so as not to alarm the competition. Once they had a foothold then that was the time to beat the drum. Marketing and distribution had already been arranged through one of the lesser known companies that was pleased to get the account without demanding outrageous margins. Thruways Brewery only had to focus on production giving a spread of risk suiting both Ranger Inc. and Anthony.

'The contract details had been mutually checked and agreed so there is nothing further to do except sign the contracts that are, of course, conditional to the finalisation of the Thruways Brewery sale' Anthony nodded ' and then there is the other proposal that you made that we have considered.' Again Anthony just nodded, deciding it's better to keep quiet and let Richard Parker play his cards.

'We have agreed in principle to purchasing twenty five percent of the Thruways Brewery for the proposed one million pounds, except that we have amended the terms from the funds being paid up front to half being paid after the successful delivery of the first months supply and the second half of the funds being paid after the second month successful delivery. Furthermore, the full amount is to be reimbursed if at anytime during the first year the company or the supply fails for whatever reason. To this end we will take out a lien against the assets. Its all in the contract.' Richard passed three copies of the contract to Anthony.

Anthony whilst not showing any emotion was annoyed at the change in terms as he had counted on the one million for the initial payment for the purchase of the Thruways Brewery. He would now have to raise the shortfall by other means. How dare Ranger Inc. change his proposal! He took it as a direct criticism of his ability and integrity.

However, they had him between a rock and a hard place. He needed their contract not only for cash flow but also to give the business credence. He had to accept these terms, as even though the sale of the Ortan brewery land was completed beforehand the initial payment was for his coffers not for the purchase of Thruways.

'That seems perfectly reasonable Richard' Anthony lied 'I have no problem in signing the contracts now if that's convenient.' Anthony needed to have this contract in place to ensure he could raise the bridging finance. He didn't really want Ranger in at all but the benefits outweighed the negatives and he certainly needed them now, especially to raise a loan.

The Ranger Inc. contract was signed and just short of two weeks the bridging finance was in place that allowed the one million to be paid to complete the purchase of Thruways Brewery giving Anthony seventy five percent ownership.

'I want you to notify the master brewer from Ortan that he is being transferred to Thruways Brewery and here is a list of five other staff that will be transferred, the rest will be let go.' Toby Thornton looked bewildered.

I don't understand, who is going to run Ortan's production?'

'No one as the production of Farcet Mill Ale will be handled by Thruways. The rest of the products have already been dropped as you know.'

'So when is this happening?' Toby was still confused.

'Today Toby, as I have bought Thruways Brewery in conjunction with Ranger Inc. Thruways will produce Farcet Mill and Ranger's Passmore along with everything else it has on its books which will make Thruways a very profitable business.'

'So Ortan will cease production leaving it with no business and only the land and assets of any value. What do you have in mind then, to sell up?' Anthony decided that it was not the right time to tell Toby that there were no assets or land in Ortan Brewery.

'Look, get the staff transfers out of the way and I'll discuss the rest with you later.' Toby's head reeled, too many unknowns and why must I do the dirty work he thought. Anthony wasn't about to tell him that after the staff transfer and dismissals Ortan Brewery Ltd would be just an empty shell with a bad reputation making his shares and options worthless.

Anthony drove home entering through the automatic security gate, admiring the beauty of Farcet Hall that was worth every penny spent. The whole of Peterborough was impressed which was the outcome Anthony had aimed for. The image was complete and negated the complaining of those he had trod on, sending many to ruin and despair. This was something Anthony took an unconscious pleasure in, as surely they indeed deserved everything they got. He had the means and power to control others and achieve what he needed to build his personal wealth and standing.

'Hello stranger, busy day?' Julie was preparing their dinner. The children were in bed and staff had gone home several hours ago so all was quiet. Anthony juniour had been born exactly twenty-four months after Karen, to the day, after an unexpected and uneventful pregnancy much to the annoyance of Anthony and the delight of Julie. They employed a second au pair to ensure twenty-four hour support for Julie. The proposal that Anthony should have a vasectomy was received with disbelief and anger, as it was Julie's responsibility to ensure she didn't fall pregnant again or else it would mean an abortion without discussion.

'Yes, a very fruitful day overall so all good at the moment.' Anthony poured himself a red wine.

'Wine?' Anthony asked Julie.

'Not just yet as just finishing a G & T. I'll have one with dinner though.' He never asked her about her day as to be honest he never thought about it, given life was all about him. Julie sighed, but then again he kept her in comfort and her allowance was substantial so small price to pay she thought. They ate their dinner in the dining room as Anthony always insisted even though Julie would have preferred to sit at the kitchen table for convenience really but again she kept the peace, avoiding one of his tantrums. His incessant drinking was taking its toll on his health with dark mood swings becoming more frequent.

'There is a riding stable I have been visiting just out of town, mainly to stand in for the senior instructor from time to time.'

'With the horses and stables here I'd have thought you could run your own riding school.'

'You know I need to develop my dressage and show jumping skills Anthony. Anyway there isn't enough room. I also like to teach, which gives me an interest.' Julie had been waiting for the opportunity to discuss her new venture and as he was reasonably relaxed now was the time.

'You have the children to give you an interest.'

'I know and they are more than an interest of course. However, I need to get out and about to meet other like-minded women. Have a bit of fun, socialise you know.'

'You could always get a job' he retorted cruelly 'How are you going to balance the children, riding school and running the house. Seems a bit ambitious to me.' Anthony poured himself another wine, his third, emptying the bottle while looking across to the sideboard to the second bottle he had brought up from the cellar. Julie was still on her first and last small glass.

'Glad you brought that up' Julie would need to tread carefully 'as I have asked Janet to start later so she can prepare dinner for us Monday through to Thursday. Of course I would need another au pair to manage the children and as George and Felicity don't need their au pair it would be an opportunity to take on a tried and proven person don't you think?'

'I didn't even know George and Felicity had an au pair.' He liked George and Felicity as they paid him due respect and acknowledged his achievements. Anthony's success came at the sacrifice of others or so the rumours would have it.

'Are you paying for the au pair?'

'No, you can put her on the Thruways books like everyone else here.' Even I'm on the books thought Julie. She was rattled, keep calm, play the game and let him get in his cutting remarks, make it difficult for everyone, treat her like he treated everyone else other than those he had a use for or who he perceived were on an equal footing. Julie knew his personal wealth and earnings were substantial and she enjoyed the trips to London and overseas holidays that were becoming more frequent. New York was her favourite although they usually ended drinking and eating too much starting each day in a jaded and seedy state that could only be rectified by a bottle of champagne for lunch. She hated that aspect of it. She knew he would never scrimp on these sorties, as he needed to exhibit his wealth and standing, behaviour just short of flamboyant that the 'old money' rightfully interpreted as the actions of the nouveau riche that failed to impress. Money talks, wealth whispers was the idiom that was incomprehensible to Anthony.

'As you always say darling, impressions are important and our standing in the community has to be seen as above those who purport to be equal. Its good for your business dealings isn't it' Julie pulled out the ace and Anthony begrudgingly buckled.

Ortan Brewery Limited was finally finished, with everything transferred to Thruways Brewery except the land that had been sold with the proceeds going straight into Anthony's business account. Simon had agreed to come across as managing director of Thruways. Anthony was pleased that Simon had stepped up to the mark proving he was more than capable although a little idealistic. He had to be mentored on the business side something Anthony had to keep an eye on to ensure the end result was in the best interest for himself. All settled to a very lucrative routine for Anthony although he didn't get involved in the day to day running of the brewery.

'What are we going to do about selling the assets of Ortan Brewery?' Toby had poured a pint of Farcet Hall Ale for Anthony who was sitting at his usual bar stool in the White Swan. Anthony took a long draw of the ale.

'There are no assets Toby, as Ortan brewery doesn't have any assets.' Anthony said in a matter of fact way.

'What do you mean, no assets?' Toby was confused.

'The land was purchase by my personal company and the plant and machinery purchased by Thruways Brewery. Furthermore, the land has since been sold to developers leaving Ortan Brewery Limited a shell company, which you will appreciate is owned by me." Anthony was emotionless.

'Where does that leave me then? Surely I have to receive at least 5% of the sale of the land and assets at the very least.' Toby was calculating.

Anthony reached into his pocket for loose change and took a fifty pence piece placing it on the counter.

'There you are, your total revenue from the eleven pound sale proceeds. Don't forget to declare it to the tax man.' Anthony laughed.

'You sold the land and assets for eleven pounds!' Toby Shrieked

Anthony walked out of the White Swan into the cool evening air with a feeling of contentment at having turned a basket case brewery into a lucrative development site while moving assets of any worth into Thruways Brewery, that he had restructured into a going concern, his cash cow for years to come. On the way he had increased his personal cash and assets wealth substantially, all without spending his own money. Those who suffered along the way were inconsequential.

❖

Toby Thornton sat in the small office next to the disorganised and dusty storeroom at the rear of the White

Swan. He stared at the wall with unseeing eyes as he tried to take stock and make some sense of what had just happened and where that left him in the scheme of things. He hated Anthony Drax with a vengeance not only for what he had just done but also for sucking him into his web a lies and deceit that led him to do his dirty work. Actually he had always hated Anthony, the slimy well-dressed good-looking condescending bastard who attracted women and flashed the cash while screwing anything and every body both literally and figuratively to build his empire and wealth.

Most of all he hated himself. He knew he was as dodgy as they come without the brutality of Anthony although he was always on the take with borderline morals and ethics to boot. He realised while he had just stayed afloat most of his life he was always looking for the pot of gold at the end of the rainbow which had proved to be evasive. Why couldn't he have learnt a trade or got some sort of profession with a secure career building to a retirement package but he also knew that was not within his psyche such a mundane and boring existence. He couldn't have done it.

In essence he had lost the very little he had through his greed which led him into the Drax trap. Fuck, fuck, fuck! He had even lost his fifty percent equity stake in the White Swan, how could he have been so stupid as it was his retirement fund, his pension. At least Helen still had her half of the White Swan so all was not lost and he had a paid position as manager. Toby was trying to salvage what was left. How many others did Anthony screw over? Toby knew of quite a few here in Peterborough even in the relatively short time Anthony had been here. Undoubtedly there must be many dotted all over who would like to see Anthony fall on his sword. How could he have been so dumb to have fired Anthony's bullets as he knew it had more than sullied his reputation as the patrons who he fired from Ortan Brewery moved away from the White Swan to drink in other pubs as reflected in his weekly takings. God, can it get any worse.

Toby locked the office and walked back to the bar.

'Katherine, I need to have an early evening as not feeling too bright to tell the truth.'

'Okay Toby.' Katherine was the bar manager and lived on the premises with her sixteen year old daughter Beryl. Toby thought Beryl was a terrible name to have called a baby, what was she thinking.

'Just a bit tired, catch you in the morning, are you alright to lock up?'

'Fine Toby, take care and see you in the morning.'

The air was cool and still as Toby walked to his car in a dejected mood knowing that he was hanging on by the skin of his teeth. He arrived home to a small bungalow that was fortunately in Helen's name. As usual she had left his supper covered in foil in the oven, a snack really as he usually had an early dinner at the pub. He couldn't face anything to eat though. He made a cup of tea and went into the lounge where Helen was watching television.

'Your home early.' Helen said without any real interest.

'Draining day, more than usual.' He slumped in his well worn lounge chair.

The television chatted away with bursts of canned laughter trying to give some inane game show the semblance of intelligence. Toby was lost in his own thoughts and heard little.

'Toby! Toby!'

Toby was jolted out of his thoughts.

'What is it Helen?' he looked surprised.

Helen muted the television.

'We need to talk Toby.'

They hadn't talked in months so why do we need to talk now Toby thought.

'I'm leaving you Toby and going to live with my sister in Norwich. I am selling my fifty percent of the White Swan and already have a buyer plus I am putting the house up for sale.'

Toby laughed, a loud and raucous laugh that was totally out of context for the situation. Helen was startled and thought that he had finally flipped his lid. What's this guy about she said to herself?

'Not the response I expected Toby.' Helen looked at Toby with distaste and wondered why she hadn't left him years ago.

'Sorry Helen, its just that I was saying to myself a while ago that things couldn't get worse, so you have to see the funny side surely.' Toby chuckled again at the turn of events. He got up and went to the kitchen fridge for a can of beer then went back to the lounge.

'So you are going to live with Stephanie then.' He didn't mind Stephanie. 'Why do we have to put the house up for sale?' It didn't really bother him that Helen was leaving him although they had never talked about it he knew it was inevitable. Perhaps they should have done it years ago he thought.

'We don't. You can buy me out for a hundred and fifty thousand which the average of the three valuations there on the bureau.'

'You know I don't have the money.'

'Exactly and that's why it will be put up for sale. Actually my fifty percent equity in the White Swan has already been sold.'

'You have been a busy little girl.' Helen was always more organised and efficient.

She wasn't going to be drawn into a discussion. They were both tired of it all and lacked any emotion.

'What's this about the sale of your equity in the White Swan.' Toby was curious.

'You could have bought it but I knew you didn't have the money.'

'Your right there, so who is the mystery buyer?'

'Anthony Drax.'

Again, Toby launched into uncontrolled laughter. He should have guessed that Anthony would approach Helen, whom he had and it was this that made up Helen's mind to leave Toby.

'Well done you but make sure he puts the money in the bank first before you do the deal.' Toby didn't care anymore, as he didn't have the strength to argue or be angry.

'The two hundred thousand pounds is already in the bank with all documents signed and sealed. I had my solicitor handle it. At least you have your half of the White Swan.'

Toby giggled uncontrollably. He didn't know she had a solicitor. So she got two hundred thousand pounds from that swine Drax who stiffed him for one hundred thousand pounds the slimy sod but then again Anthony had him over a barrel.

Helen went to bed while Toby sat in the lounge drinking until he fell asleep about three in the morning.

Helen had left for work when he woke on the sofa with a dry mouth and thumping head. He had felt the worse though during his long drinking career.

Toby made some coffee and toast showered and dressed. He was late.

Katherine was working in the bar when Toby arrived and Beryl had left for work at the local shoe shop where she had been since she left school at fifteen. There was an air of change something seemed different somehow.

'Morning Katherine.' Toby felt a bit seedy but he would have coffee and some breakfast when the cook arrived even an early pint would sort him out.

'Mr Drax is waiting for you in the office Toby.' Toby's head snapped around to look at Katherine.

'How long has he been here?'

'Since eight Toby.'

Anthony strode into the public lounge immaculately dress and groomed as usual.

'Sit down over here Toby.' Anthony ordered.

Katherine brought two coffees.

'So you own the White Swan outright.' Toby said lamely.

'Not only that Toby but I have appointed Katherine as manager, given you will no longer be working here. I'll have your personal effects delivered to your house this afternoon.' Anthony picked up his coffee went back to the office. Toby walked out of the White Swan for the last time.

Helen settled in with her sister Stephanie who lived in a fully modernised grade two listed eighteen century four bedroom vicarage something she had bought with her husband of thirty years one year prior to his sudden death. They would spend the rest of their lives with each other in comfort enjoying the quiet countryside just south of Norwich.

It was during the third week in her new residence that she received a phone call from the authorities in Peterborough informing her that Toby's body had been found in woods half a mile from the White Swan. He had hung himself. Only five people attended his funeral including Helen and Stephanie. There was no sign of Anthony Drax.

11

'What is your agenda for the week?' Not that Anthony really cared what Julie did with her time as long as it didn't impinge on his life.

'The usual.' Julie responded impassively.

The afternoon sun was trapped where they sat on the south west side of the house patio. In fact the sun was quite hot. Julie sipped on her cool lemon water while Anthony finished a second beer.

'What does the usual involve these days.' He reached into the coolbox for another beer.

'I am preparing for a dressage competition next month at Addington Equestrian.' Julie was looking forward to getting away for a week. She tolerated Anthony's loutish behaviour of drunkenness and infidelity on a regular basis. The children were well into their teens with both of them boarding at private school. She looked at Anthony realising for the umpteenth time, not only wasn't she in love with him but a steady growing dislike had developed into distaste. She had developed an unhealthy distance to the man who had lost his self-respect and was in a dark place of depression and anger. There were no positive feelings left, just pity for this sorrowful person.

'What about yourself?' She didn't care as to what he did or didn't do as long as he provided for the family. Thank God for Simon, a competent manager of Thruways Brewery, the real provider for all.

'The usual.' Smirked Anthony. She didn't respond. 'You certainly have it made my dear, riding on my shirttails but then that's what women tend to do, don't you think?' Julie refused to take the bait. He couldn't help it, as he had to turn a pleasant afternoon into something distasteful.

Anthony looked at Julie and wondered who she really was. The beer was working its magic on his seediness from the previous evening. He didn't like her, this opportunist taking advantage of his good will, bringing nothing to the marriage, not a penny had she contributed. He decided to contact Sandy Milford to review his Will that left most of his estate to Julie with provision for the children, be damned if she should receive anything he mused as he reached into the coolbox.

Farcet Hall had been well established for some time and was the crowning jewel for Anthony, his castle and sanctuary. The stables had been refurbished with everything sitting comfortably within the extensive six-foot new build stonewall. Landscaping tastefully carried out with small areas of gardens accessed by interconnecting lawn paths fringed with a Piet Odulf perennial meadow bringing the natural environment to areas that could easily have become too formal; such as the original restored knot garden that was separated from the south-facing front of Farcet Hall by the gravel drive. The grounds boasted a rotund enjoyed at summer garden parties spilling out into the numerous comfortable seating areas between it and the Hall. Outbuildings had been meticulously restored for guest accommodation and the main storage shed converted into a garage large enough for the small fleet of vehicles Anthony collected.

The stables housed the eighteen horses Julie had bought with assistance from Ruben Fitzroy who owned Fitzroy

Stables some five miles south of Farcet Hall. Ruben had taken over the family stables from his father François Fritz Roi from Normandy anglicised to Francis Fitzroy. Francis married Anne Villiers and their only child was Ruben. Ruben grew into a handsome six-foot typically fine boned thin Frenchman well proportioned physic strengthened from years of working with horses at the Stables. He had been schooled in France and England having graduated from Oxford University with a degree in mathematics. He of course spoke fluent French and English as well as German and Spanish. As Julie had found out during the purchase of the livestock for her stables Ruben was conservative in conversation, not that he was unfriendly but he couldn't see the point of entering into inane waffle just for the sake of talking. He and Julie got on well developing a respectable friendship that seemed to be a natural progression without any other agenda from either of them.

Julie didn't discuss Ruben with Anthony. Anthony wasn't interested in horses anyway. Although he had toyed with the idea of having a racehorse more as a status symbol than a genuine interest in racing. Ruben had never talked about his personal or social circumstances and Julie never asked him although the general gossip among her girlfriends indicated that although he had several long-term relationships he had never married. He spent extended periods in France where he had various business interests and farming assets. This enigmatic Frenchman was well liked and respected while supplying the women at their G&T afternoons with ample fodder for speculation.

Much had changed on the Drax front with the children growing up too fast. Relationships with the children were comfortable and with Thruways Brewery keeping Anthony busy while providing an enviable lifestyle they had all become accustomed to. Even though their relationship was distant they still had the traditional yearly trip to New York where Anthony regularly took every opportunity to distastefully boast his wealth failing to impress due to his crass belligerent manner. The New Yorkers brushed him off as one of the nouveau riche Englishmen who over indulged disgracefully. Anthony had purchased a holiday house in Palma, Mallorca, one of the Balearic Islands off the east coast of Spain, more as an escape for Anthony than Julie who didn't enjoy the place at all. Anthony tended to visit regularly on his own where he had befriended some British expats who lived there permanently. They were all heavy drinkers with Anthony taking excess to a new level that even his new found drinking friends found awe inspiring and impossible to compete with. They kidded him that the time he spent in England was for respite.

It was when Karen and Anthony entered secondary school that they tended to want to go to Palma on every available holiday with Julie and Anthony. Julie begrudgingly complied although after several disasters stipulated only one trip each year.

❖

On the second day of the dressage competitions at Addington Equestrian, Julie prepared her Irish sport horse Irish Rose or Rosie for short, a sleek shiny black Irish beauty backed by an impressive pedigree. She had a good temperament, being calm, yet lively when needed, and was very tough indeed. Julie adored Rosie and was sure the feeling was mutual as they were good friends who became one with Julie in the saddle. Their success was moderate however although progress was in the right direction.

'Bonjour Julie puis-je aider?'

Startled, Julie looked up to see the wide beautiful smile from Ruben.

'Bien sûr monsieur' Julie responded. 'What are you doing here Ruben?'

It was at this very moment that Julie had conscious recognition of what had been simmering in her subconscious ever since she had met Ruben. She felt warm and pleased to see him. He was everything that Anthony wasn't. Her feelings for Ruben would remain her secret.

'I came over to see a client and noticed on the your name on the competitor listing, so decided to search you out. How are you Julie?'

'Actually, I am very well and enjoying the competition although our performance leaves a little to be desired. And you?'

'Très bien merci, never better, pleased to get away from the stables for a while. Rosie is certainly a beauty. I am sure there are great things to come from you two.' Ruben genuinely appreciated the qualities of both females and their skills.

'Sorry Ruben but I have to get going as my next event is due shortly.'

'No problems Julie, any chance of catching up later?'

'Are you staying over?' She was surprised.

'Yes, just for the night due to a late afternoon meeting with my client. I booked into Winslow Hall.

'Me too, for the week though, I have to sort Rosie out in her stable first, so may be a little late for catching up.' Julie knew she would be tired and had a busy week planned.

'I have booked a table at the restaurant so you're welcome to join me if your not too tired. What do you say?' He is considerate thought Julie.

'I would love to Ruben but will need an early night. Need my beauty sleep I'm afraid.'

'Okay, lets make it eight in the restaurant.' Refusing to take no for an answer Ruben gave a slight wave and strode off leaving Julie to get on with preparing Rosie.

Julie walked into the restaurant where Ruben was seated on the small sofa just inside and left of the main door. He stood to greet her.

'Our table is over there near the window.' Ruben led the way.

Once seated the waiter came over with the menus.

'Would you like to order drinks?' The waiter took out his pen and note pad.

'Julie?'

'Lime and soda please.'

'Make that two.' Ruben was not a big drinker and quite thirsty so a non-alcoholic drink would hit the spot. Julie raised her eyebrows as to start a meal without alcohol being ordered was a first, something Anthony would never have contemplate. They both ordered a light main course then settled back with their drinks.

'How did your meeting go Ruben?'

'Very good, the guy is from Northampton and wants me to agist four of his horses and to carry out basic racing training for one of them. Could turn out to be a lucrative deal as he is well heeled. I have been toying with the idea to resurrect the training circuit that has lain idle since my father passed away. Perhaps its time.'

'Good for you Ruben onwards and upwards as they say.'

They chatted as they ate their meal about the competition and Julie's prospects which according to her were not that exciting as she was in it for the experience and to be with her riding friends who provided a welcome relief from Farcet Hall daily routine. Ruben noticed that Julie was flagging so suggested to call it a night, a welcome suggestion for Julie.

'Julie, before you go I have a proposition for you.' Julie looked at him blankly.

'Would you consider a position as the senior instructor with the Fitzroy Riding School?'

Julie looked up in surprise 'We should talk about this later please Ruben as I'm shattered to tell you the truth. I'll come over next week to discuss if that's alright with you?'

'Of course, I should have been more considerate. Go get some sleep and I'll see you next week. Goodnight.'

'Thanks for the meal and good night. I'll see you next week. Take care.'

The rest of the week went quickly in the hustle and bustle of the organised equestrian events and catching up with friends she had developed over the years within the equestrian crowd. No hidden agenda, just a common interest with a lashing of competitiveness made for an interesting week of much needed respite from the dysfunctional Anthony Drax. It was only when Julie was driving back to Farcet Hall in her Citroen Jumper horse transporter, the smaller of the two transporters she owned, that she appreciated how much stress had been shed from her body and mind. As she got closer to home she could feel the tension returning. After her dinner with Ruben he had only touched her mind once or twice however driving home on this balmy afternoon she smiled allowing rare inner flirtatious thoughts about this well dressed rather handsome and incredibly courteous well mannered Frenchman. He was so refreshing the antithesis of Anthony she thought, immediately hating herself for thinking so but it was true so why shouldn't she indulge. It could have been so different but then again she went in eyes wide open appreciating the risks of marrying a person like Anthony. Was it worth it? Julie wasn't sure it was and yet she couldn't conceive a life without Anthony or Karen and her lifestyle was very attractive. With little feeling for Anthony she had learnt to manage his insatiable ego while keeping in the shadows without upsetting the apple cart. Their love life was non-existent with physical contact a distant memory, she shuddered. Anthony had let himself go both physically and mentally developing an overweight puffiness and although he kept himself clean and well dressed it didn't disguise the smell of alcohol. He struggled with a perpetual seediness and deteriorating health, it is so sad, Julie reflected.

'Good morning Ruben' it was the second week after Julie had returned 'apologies for not getting in touch with you last week.' She had finally found time to call.

'No need to apologise Julie we are all very busy these days. How are you?'

'Fine, would it be possible to come over to discuss the instructor position you proposed?'

'Of course, would tomorrow be convenient for you?'
'As long as it's before three pm as I have to go to town.'
'Look, why don't you come over at twelve for an early lunch?'
'That sounds civilised, would love to.'
'That's settled then. I'll look forward to catching up with you Julie. Bye.'
'Bye.'

Anthony had decided to take up an offer to join several acquaintances in Scotland to stalk and shoot deer while Julie was at Addington Equestrian so caught the train to Waverley Station, Edinburgh where he was picked up and driven to the not too shabby accommodation of the hunting lodge. He didn't have any close friends, only acquaintances.

It wasn't that people didn't valued his intellect or his friendship, it was his money and novelty factor that made him tolerable. The organisers of such an event used him as a stopgap when someone pulled out at the last minute, even then this would only occur when the rest of the clients were the moneyed, boozy, loud and boisterous type. Strangely, it was Anthony's belligerence and awe inspiring drinking ability that kept even the hardiest drinker of the group somewhat subdued and in check. Most of these clients had shared a hunt with Anthony before and were cautious of his inclination to avoid paying for anything if possible and not to get involved in any betting challenge he may propose as Anthony was street wise enough to fleece the unsuspecting. For the organisers it was about business so their clients were required to pay in advance for the week's activities.

They hunted but were only marginally successful due to the late afternoon and evening heavy drinking that left them jaded most mornings. A full English breakfast and copious amounts of coffee usually had them reasonably sober and focussed to stalk for a few hours until the process was repeated the next day. By the end of the week these not so young clients were exhausted and bleary eyed to such an extent that the organisers refused to take them on the last day mystery hunt that was expected by most other clients who managed themselves and their behaviour befitting the gentry the organisers preferred.

Anthony slept on the train to Peterborough and by the time he arrived home he was shattered so took himself to bed in his private room so as not to be disturbed Julie when she came home. He realised he hadn't thought about Julie at all while away but then again why should he?

Julie pulled her Land Rover to a stop in front of Fitzroy House a nineteenth century red brick understated building that looked rustic yet somehow sophisticated with its slate roof and patches of loosely cropped ivy giving that cottagey look to something too large to be a cottage.

Ruben opened the right side of the ancient weathered oak doors that led into the large foyer and descended the three steps to the drive. He wore a pair of Emporio Armani jeans that hung on his hips with a dark grey flannel work shirt tucked in, well worn brown leather belt and work boots were contradicted by his well groomed hair and aviator sun glasses. He greeted Julie with a warm and friendly smile as she alighted from the car. I bet he would look good dressed in flour sacks she thought.

'Hello Mrs Drax.'

'That's a very formal greeting Mr Fitzroy.'
'Well this could very well be a serious business meeting you know. Lunch first though.'
He ushered Julie around to the side of the house where in a small-secluded sun trap a patio table had been tastefully set for lunch. They sat down as Julie put on her sunglasses against the midday glare on this warm dreamy day tempered by a light slightly cool breeze keeping the heat at bay.
Ruben poured two glasses of ice water adding a slice of lemon.
'There you are.' He handed a glass to Julie.
'Cheers.' They said in unison as they clinked glasses.
Mrs Tucker came out through the adjoining kitchen door with two large Caesar salads. They took their time playing with their food while they chatted about anything other than work in a relaxed and congenial environment. It has been so long since I have enjoyed myself so much thought Julie.
'Right Julie, lets go down to the office at the stables and I'll go over what I have in mind to see what you think.
'You know how the riding school works given the amount of time you have assisted. What I am planning to do is double the capacity and recruit two more instructors giving five in total.' Julie listened carefully. 'However, I will also need to recruit a manager and that's where you come in. When you're away on holiday or whatever I can stand in. Obviously it will mean that you will need to commit to the position and give the required time to make it work. What do you think?'

'Quite a bit to take in Ruben, I'll need to give it some thought. There are a few questions I need to ask first.'

They talked for several hours while they wandered around the expansive stables where the staff were busy with grooming, maintenance and exercising the horses, many of them client owned and hopefully to be trained by Ruben for the race events on the calendar. He had finally resurrected this side of the business.

'One last thing Julie, if you decided to come on board one option is to be my partner in the riding school business, as such you will be paid a handsome retainer with a half share in the profits. Furthermore, the riding school will sit in a separate limited company so the opportunity will be there for you to enter a share option scheme.' Ruben had prepared two copies of an agreement giving both to Julie.

'Take these home to go through them, get legal advice if appropriate and let me know what how you feel.'

Julie was a little overwhelmed but knew she would have to consider everything in fine detail before committing or otherwise.

'Thanks Ruben, I will do exactly that and get back to you as soon as possible. I do appreciate the lunch and would like you to thank Mrs Tucker for me please. Now, I need to be heading off.'

They said their goodbyes and Julie drove quietly away as Ruben looked after her.

What an interesting and thoughtful person Ruben thought as he watched the Land Rover disappear down the drive, no one had ever thought to thank Mrs Tucker for lunch before. He loved Mrs Tucker as only a little boy could love his nanny who had lived as part of the Fitzroy family for fifty years, ever since she came to them as a young woman.

❖

The Fitzroy Riding School had been in operation for eighteen months since Julie had come on board as a full partner and director with fifty percent of the shares being granted as options to her at an attractive nominal exercise rate. She assisted Ruben with the recruiting of the extra two staff, otherwise she was free to run, manage and develop the business as she saw fit. Ruben was pleased that Julie was serious and diligent ensuring he was kept in the loop at all times. She was business savvy and had taken this business from sleepy hollow to a vibrant growing enterprise that impressed Ruben greatly. Julie and Ruben's relationship was very much on a platonic basis making them well-suited business partners within a burgeoning friendship. There was not an inkling of inappropriate behaviour from either and if truth were known they genuinely shared a deep and caring love that was too complicated to even discuss. They were enjoying what they were doing and the time spent together. For Julie it was something she needed and enjoyed, especially when the children were away at school and Anthony was out doing whatever it was he was doing.

When Julie had told Anthony that she was going into partnership with Ruben he was furious and they broke into a row that was fortunately short lived. Julie refused to prolong any senseless argument. The bitch, I'll sort her out. Anthony reached for his phone.
'Sandy, I need to see you as soon as possible.'

'Hello Anthony, good to talk to you.' Sandy Milford laughed, Anthony didn't.

'It's going to have to be in three weeks Anthony as I will be in New Zealand visiting my daughter and new son in law. I need some rest and recreation as well given a busy year so far. What's it about?'

'Several things I need to sort out.' He couldn't give a toss about Sandy's trip, as it was an inconvenience. 'Let's fix a date for when you return. You obviously don't have any consideration for your clients.'

Anthony fantasised that Julie was having an affair with Ruben, more a projection of his behaviour. She must be as she wasn't interested in having sex with him, let alone sleep in the same bed. Fuck, who does she think she is but that will change Mrs Drax, I can assure you.

Anthony was bored so as usual spent every opportunity encouraging acquaintances whether it be the bank manager, past business associates, any unsuspecting academic, local dignitary or person of standing to engage with him over dinner or most often a luncheon. As his drinking was legendary many people took up the offer just to witness the phenomenon. Rarely did they accept the offer a second time as most were cajoled into keep pace ending in an inebriated state that they neither wanted nor needed. Conversation from the egocentric Anthony was totally about his wealth, Thruways Brewery, Farcet Hall or latest holiday including how much he spent on alcohol that for some bizarre reason he thought was a gauge to the success of the holiday and would impress the listener. Consequently, his aberrant behaviour was a well-established topic of conversation at dinner parties and for those who knew him best, a standard joke.

His belligerent behaviour spilled over into his visits to Thruways Brewery as the owner and chairman he could do what he wanted.

'Why are you having so much difficulty in increasing output of the brewery?' Anthony knew why.

'You know why' Simon had been over this a dozen times before but his father never ceased to raise the matter 'we are near capacity so if you want production to be increased by meaningful volumes then we will need capital investment. To warrant such investment we will need to have fixed and secure demand such as a take or pay agreement from new clients'

'Why haven't you got any new clients then or more sales?' Anthony spat the words. He knew Simon was his best asset and unlike himself, a good businessman. He also knew that he had his son trapped in the business giving him a false sense of security for his future while he toyed with Simon's positive nature and good will that generated no respect from Anthony as he saw it a weakness more than anything.

Simon sighed.

'If that's the way you want to go then lets work it up into a financial and business model and take it to the bank for ratification then we can put the sales team on finding new clients.' His father was more often than not unreasonable and irrational as Simon knew for the umpteenth time this conversation would go nowhere. He who must be obeyed was the mantra.

'What are your projections for retained profits at the end of the year.' Anthony asked quietly. Perhaps he is getting serious thought Simon.

'Just short of three hundred thousand pounds.'

'In that case I want you to factor in a dividend payment of two hundred and fifty thousand to myself.' Anthony had had enough of Simon with his calm logical rational explanations that really could not be counteracted. He readied himself to leave the office. He loathed his son for being the businessman he could never be.

'How can you even think about expansion when you keep draining the business of profits.' Simon knew it was futile to argue.

'Listen Simon, I am not interested in what you think so keep your opinions to yourself. Do your job and I'll run the brewery.' Anthony slammed the door as he left.

Damn insolent bastard, how dare he question anything I say thought Anthony as he made his way to another boozy luncheon. By the time he was driving out of the brewery premises Simon was the furthest thing from his mind.

Simon looked at the door for a full fifteen minutes after his father had left. He felt nothing for Anthony after years of constant niggling and put-downs. There was little chance that his father would bring him in as a partner or offer him any security in the brewery. He knew he had to make the break and go his own way, something he often thought about and yet had failed to enact.

Simon was the antithesis of his father, something appreciated by staff and associates alike. Anthony was trapped into begrudgingly supporting Simon although he pushed him to limits often only because he exploited

Simon's tolerance and forgiving characteristics inherited from his mother. In fact Simon had no empathy for his father, fully understanding his pathology; he had learnt to cope with his mood swings and caustic attitudes. The only redeeming factor was that he was well remunerated with annual bonuses and fringe benefits, but required constant expressions of gratification to sooth his father's insatiable ego and narcissism.

His father would often admit, he didn't have any friends and business acquaintances were a dime a dozen and not to be trusted, so Simon was often required to accompany him on one or annual two holiday Jaunts that inevitably turned into an orgy of gluttony and excessive drinking requiring Simon to be the carer.

❖

That night, while Anthony slept, his body struggled to process the copious quantity of alcohol and fat ingested from the sumptuous luncheon with his bank manager. Years of abuse had taken its toll and no amount of exercise or the long-term drug regime prescribed by his general practitioner, Doctor Murray, would help this evening. He had not bothered Doctor Murray with the reoccurring angina attacks he wrongfully put down to indigestion that seemed to respond to the constant use of antacids. His heart's blood vessels were clogged, slowing the supply of blood to this critical heart muscle until on this particular night one of the vessels became occluded by a small blood clot, which formed while blood slowed trying to force its way through the small atherosclerotic gap of fatty tissue within the artery that had been laid down over decades of excess. In turn the heart muscle was starved of oxygenated blood and in its struggle caused fibrillation of the right ventricle, enough to form a larger clot from this sluggish thick congested and polluted blood. The new clot was on a mission as it was catapulted out of the right ventricle through the lungs into the aorta finding its way through the Carotid Artery into the Basilar Artery where it lodged, starving Anthony's brain stem Pons of that precious and life giving oxygen. The consequence was sudden and irreparable damage to a large section of the brain stem leading to a state of pseudocoma. His heart survived. It was in this state that Julie found Anthony at seven thirty in the morning, within forty-five minutes he was in Peterborough City Hospital and by three thirty that afternoon he had been transported to the stroke unit at the Hospital of St John in St Johns Wood, London.

He would never keep his appointment with Sandy.

It was the informed opinion of the stroke specialist that Anthony, although not brain dead, was severely incapacitated due to the anoxic state rendering him oblivious to anything that surrounded him. In short he was in a persistent vegetative state. The specialist wrote a diagnosis report to this effect and issued it to Julie for the family. The prognosis was anything but encouraging. The only course of action was for Julie to take Anthony home and provide twenty-four hour nursing care. The long-term outcome was seemingly dire for all, more so for Anthony.

The cavernous main bedroom at Farcet Hall with its equally sumptuous en suite was converted into a hospital type accommodation for Anthony who would be cared for by the four full time stroke nurses employed specifically for the task of twenty four hour care seven days a week.

Every piece of technology needed to monitor Anthony's signs was installed with no expense spared.

Julie was surprised at how quickly and easy the routine of caring for Anthony was established due to the professionalism of the nurses. He was bathed in bed, regularly turned to avoid bedsores with daily physiotherapy and massages. These tasks including writing reports based on observation and the monitoring readouts kept the nurses busy which they appreciated. The room had a lounge suite for guests to relax in and a table and chairs for business meetings or discussions to take place, something that Julie insisted on as she felt all matters must be discussed in front of Anthony, out of respect.

Julie knew she had to go back to work at Fitzroy Stables more for her sanity than anything else. It was so good to be out of Farcet Hall she thought although it had only been three months since Anthony's stroke but the stress was something else. At the end of the first day Ruben took her up to the house to discuss the situation and it was then that without comment they consummated their relationship. They spent the night catching up on so much that had been neglected, a torrent of unbridled insatiable passion leaving them in an exhausted sleep until mid morning. Mrs Tucker was more than pleased. She knew it was right, Julie was right for Ruben, her Ruben.

12

'I appreciate your attendance that I suspect will be the first of many.' Julie looked at the other three people sitting at the table in front of Anthony's bed. Sandy Milford Anthony's long-term legal advisor and solicitor, Dr Cunningham from the Peterborough Hospital who had agreed to look after Anthony's health requirements and monitor his progress in conjunction with the four nurses who cared for him, Simon and Julie. The duty nurse was the only other person in the room.

'Sandy, I would be grateful if you would pick up from our last meeting and the various discussions we have had in the interim.'

'Thank you Julie, first of all if there is no objection I will record this meeting and secondly I think it would be useful if each of you would give a summary of the activities you're involved with concerning Anthony. Dr Cunningham would you mind going first?'

'Of course Mr Milford.' Reginald Cunningham was in his fifth decade and a dedicated medico who since graduating from Newcastle Medical School had devoted his life to medicine. He climbed through the ranks quickly to his current position of senior physician enjoying the status and recognition it gave him but he was good at what he did. He didn't want to go any further as he enjoyed Peterborough where he, his wife and two children were settled. Of course, opportunities came up all the time but he wasn't interested, he was happy with his lot. The fact that he had several lucrative private patients he managed outside the NHS gave him some extra income that had proven very useful. Julie had engaged Dr Cunningham to look after Anthony as a private patient.

'As we know, Anthony has suffered a severe anoxic brain stem stroke that rendered him in a vegetated state. From the monitoring and care he has been given he is very stable at the moment and I don't expect this to change in the foreseeable future.'

'What is the likelihood of Anthony regaining consciousness?' Sandy wanted to dot the i's and cross the t's, he knew he had to be thorough if what he was going to propose would stand up in court.

'Generally this is an unknown as similar cases have shown no recovery at all and yet others, rarely, have recovered consciousness as early as weeks to three or six months or more.' Reginald wasn't in the prophesying game so chose his words carefully. 'It would seem, from reading similar case studies that those who are going to recover will do so earlier than later, that is, the longer the patient is in this state the less likely he is to recover. I have covered this in depth in the medical report I gave you last week.'

'Thank you Dr Cunningham and we appreciate your report, which has been most helpful. Simon?'

When Anthony became incapacitated the relief for Simon was palpable, something that shocked him, as he realised just how much constant stress his father caused. No longer did he have to look over his shoulder, jump each time the phone rang or wondered when the door opened if it would be his father sober, drunk or sporting a hangover. Either way he would invariably be obnoxious looking to pick him up on some trivia or inane matter of no consequence.

'As I have said in the report I wrote for last week, the brewery is running well as can be expected with any issues I have I discuss with Julie. However, there are reporting and legal matters that my father handled as the owner of the business that cannot be carried out by anyone else. There is also the matter of the operating account that I have authorisation over and when funds are getting low my father tops them up from the main account that only he has authorisation over. I am approaching that critical stage where the operating account needs to be topped up or else we will be forced to close shop.' Simon had been through this before with Sandy and Julie.

'Thank you Simon, Julie?'

'Similar to the business really in that I need access to Anthony's accounts as he handled the household bills and general payments such as car insurance, employee wages and the stable costs and so on, so I am at a critical stage as everyone is working but fast approaching funding difficulties are causing concern.' Julie looked over to where Anthony lay without movement of any kind throughout this discussion. There was not a flicker of recognition that anything was taking place, so sad she thought, although she felt nothing for the man himself as the rift between them had been there for years now and neither had any compassion for the other. Julie was non the wiser to the measures Anthony was going to put in place with Sandy after he returned from his holiday, to punish her for her perceived insubordination and general lack of respect that had been simmering inside Anthony.

'I need to have control over every aspect of Anthony's person, health, finances, household and business interests with the authorisation to make decisions that may or may not require changes to funds and or assets at any time. We can't go on like this or we risk losing everything.' Tears rolled down her cheeks as she finished in a whisper. What a mess.

Sandy realised that Julie and Simon were looking at Anthony, waiting for him to provide the answers or direction as they were accustom to, he had always held control that could not be questioned, he who must be obeyed as they say.

'Right then' Sandy jolted their attention back to the table ' what I propose is that we apply to the court to grant Julie a Lasting Absolute Power of Attorney for Anthony and Simon be appointed as an agent to handle the brewery and Dr Cunningham an agent to handle Anthony's health. Julie will handle everything else while overseeing you Simon and Doctor Cunningham. What do you think?'

They discussed concerns and details of the proposal for close to an hour before they were comfortable with the concept and agreed that Sandy should seek the court's approval. Sandy refused the suggestion that he be appointed as an agent to handle all legal aspects and said he would do this under instruction from Julie. After all, he was already the family's solicitor, so no change needed there.

The hearing took place at the Magistrates Court on Bridge Street, an uninspiring building that was purely functional and soulless as such buildings are. Julie received the conditional power of attorney requiring a review by the court at three, six and twelve months, the Conditional Period. During the review period no changes to Anthony's assets could be made, however if there was no improvement in Anthony's condition then all restrictions would be lifted after the Conditional Period and Julie would have absolute power to make any decision over Anthony's assets. The court took into account that Anthony's existing Will left the majority of his estate to Julie with the residual split equally among his four children. When the Conditional Period had expired the Court ruled that even though Anthony was not legally dead his Last Will and Testament would be executed. Julie ensured she read the decision of the court in full detail to Anthony, as she was adamant that he be fully informed of anything that impacted on his life even if he was unable to comprehend.

❖

Eighteen months after the stroke, it was decided by the family that it would be in Anthony's best interest for him to move into Meadows Care Home on the outskirts of Peterborough. His dedicated nurses went with him to ensure continuity. His condition had not changed yet he lived on having lost excess weight and puffiness that accompanied excesses of alcohol and with constant movement and physiotherapy he actually looked quite healthy. It was a period of change all round as Julie now having absolute lasting power of attorney over everything to do with Anthony including his assets. She sat quietly with Anthony setting out her plans to gift enough of his shares to give Simon controlling ownership of Thruways Brewery. The residual shares are to be distributed equally between Anthony's remaining three children and Julie. Simon will have the option to purchase these shares if they are ever put up for sale. It was strange Julie thought, now that Anthony was incapacitated how she felt certain empathy for him. This stranger, this living corpse whom she had known for so long and been through so much with and who had caused her and many others so much pain and grief. Like the rest of the family, the relief from control and manipulation was profound with nothing left but this halfhearted empathy, the family deserved to have a life free from his torment.

Thruways Brewery flourished under Simon's management with his expansion strategy now having been realised. He and his staff had a secure future while Peterborough had a functional brewing industry, adding to its economy and positive future. Simon married Sonia an accountant he met at a business function and they had two children who never saw their grandfather nor he them. Simon came to an agreement to exercise his option to buy out the equity belonging to the other members of the family, although it took six years.

Farcet Hall was sold and Julie went to live with Ruben Fitzroy. She used some of the proceeds to exercise the fifty percent equity option in Fitzroy Stables. They were content with their life and relationship, deciding to marry after the court granted a decree of annulment to Julie and Anthony's marriage. The wedding was a quiet family affair held at Fitzroy House on a warm summer day with everyone in fine spirits and full of admiration for the bride and groom. How times change many thought and for the better.

The White Swan was gifted to the Thornton family who sold it with proceeds going to Toby's children.

Julie visited Anthony at Meadow Care Home monthly where she held his hand while she told him of the events, happenings and outcomes of her life. She told him how well Simon was doing and that he now owned the brewery and of her relationship with Ruben and their successful personal partnership and in business as well as how well the children were doing and what their future held for them.

Apart from the original business meetings, Anthony had not received one visit since the day of his stroke.

13

It took three years to positively diagnose that Anthony was suffering Locked in Syndrome, a fate that he would have to endure for the next two years when he would unfortunately contract pneumonia and die. It was the opinion of the specialist that Anthony had been fully cognisant of every conversation, action, decision and movement that had taken place around him from the time of his stroke.

The five years he endured this state of imprisonment would have been time enough for Anthony to reflect on the deceit, cruelty and pain he had inflict upon many who had come into contact with. It was beyond his capability to conceive that he was in anyway responsible for anything other than providing for his family and amassing an enviable estate. It was during this five years stay of execution that Julie unwittingly tortured Anthony with her in depth explanations to such a degree that he developed mind-blocking mechanisms whenever she came to visit far more often than he desired. The death he prayed for was a long time coming.

Printed in Great Britain
by Amazon